The Blooming Day

PAUL FUSCA

THE BLOOMING DAY

iUniverse books may be ordered through booksellers or by contacting:

iUniverse
1663 Liberty Drive
Bloomington, IN 47403
www.iuniverse.com
844-349-9409

ISBN: 978-1-6632-3515-2 (sc)
ISBN: 978-1-6632-3520-6 (e)

Print information available on the last page.

iUniverse rev. date: 01/20/2022

CHAPTER I

The day is October 9th, 2018. The city of Velindas is constantly moving: filled streets, luxurious hotels, teenage gangs, and even apartments for those who work in the bustling capitalist society that's only embraced in such an area. Because it's in the dead center of a desert, it almost never rains in Velindas. The humidity remains low, the temperature stays high during the day and low at night, and the outskirts of the city are filled with patches of desert sand. Besides that, the shopping districts in the city are popular among tourists and feature a long variety of products from clothes to illegal prostitutes. Typically centered around the hotels, the market sectors are also crowded and constantly moving, while the business side of the city is made for people on even longer walks or people who are living their daily lives of suffering through daily work. The business streets are never as crowded as the shopping streets, but nonetheless keep busy throughout the day.

Velindas remains alive at dusk and the morning birds greet the night owls as their sleep schedules intersect. The city is constantly bustling, hotels being built to be even larger than the competitor next door. There is never a dull moment in Velindas, whether you're taking the zipline between the two Velindas Grand Hotels that neighbor each other or taking a bite out of the ridiculously expensive food that drowns you in regret the next day. The skies are an industrial black when it's late and a glowing shade of blue in the heat of the day. Outside the vast city, there are long chains of mountains with few highways and roads to get in and out.

Velindas tends to be the city people like to fly into rather than take other means of transport, due to the beautiful desert landscape it provides by the plane's window. The sunset is more beautiful in Velindas than anywhere else, and the jazzy 80s-esque vibes are only enhanced by the late night walks. Big business buildings on one side and giant hotels and attractions for everyone to have fun with on the other describes the layout of the city, along with the dune-like outskirts. The sidewalks grow narrow by the ends of the city and once you reach the final building, it becomes a flat desert with mountains just barely walking distance away for the average person.

Velindas is home to many people, good or bad, black or white, rich or poor, but it's also home to the world's most notorious gang: Rose, an elite group of thieves numbered one through fifteen. Rose specializes in stealing the most treasured valuables they can locate, and none of their real names are known by officials. No one knows of their real identities, but they all hold supernatural abilities known as "clouds."

The concept of a cloud is similar to a superpower. One can get their own cloud naturally by genetics or by going through a life-changing experience. Such an ability can be strengthened through killing other cloud users. Clouds tend to maximize their strength in harsh situations, but using all the energy from a cloud can lead to death. Clouds can be really anything: the ability to float, the ability to see farther, the ability to see what's behind you, the ability to see through objects of your choice. There is no known limit to what a cloud can and cannot be. Some clouds are simple, like the ability to fly, and some can be bizarre, like the ability to make someone's arm move. These abilities influence the world in many ways: through gangs, through politics, through fighting, even through sports. It's estimated that 0.001% of the global population has a cloud. Despite the fact that 1 out of 100,000 people have a cloud, there is no doubt that the world is constantly changing due to these supernatural abilities.

Some clouds have a second ability, which relates to the first ability. This is known as a cloud unlock. Cloud unlocks are considered extremely rare and having one is not defined by power, but rather just the sheer nature of your cloud. Despite that fact, the more powerful a cloud is, the more likely it is to form a cloud unlock. Because clouds adapt and change to the user's will, a cloud unlock could be anything and could form at any point in a cloud's development.

The reason they're called clouds, however, is entirely up to speculation. While some historians believe clouds were associated with religion, such as a gift from God, some believe they were referred to as clouds because they are powers that are above humans. It has been argued that it's a mistranslation of a foreign language, but either way, they are known to be referred to as clouds and that's all.

Rose has been terrorizing Velindas for a few years, using the outskirts and some abandoned buildings on the outside as their hideouts. Police attempts to apprehend them have failed, and they've done whatever they wanted. The gang is wanted globally and serves as an idol to many teenage gangs. The world wants the Rose members gone, whether in jail or dead, but no one can do the job. With the world being unable to face Rose, two men enter the scene: one who seeks revenge on Rose and one who serves as a high-end detective who always solves his cases.

"You saw that calling card Rose sent us?" spoke a brown-haired individual across the room.

"What about it?" responded the blond-haired one.

"Don't you think we should be scared, Kuril? It's Rose!"

"No. It's only one of their members according to the calling card." Kuril rested his eyes. "If they try anything we have measures to make sure they don't accomplish their goal."

"I suppose you're right, but what if the—"

"Are you not a relative of the detective named Junil? Calm yourself, it's in your blood to win this one."

Time would pass across that boring room. The two men were guarding a jewel that was to be examined by a top-notch businessman in the work-side of Velindas.

"Yanni, don't you think it's a little late? We should have our visitor," Kuril wondered, "why aren't they here?"

"It sounds like you want them to come and steal the Teardrop of Alexandria. We'd be sure as hell fired," Yanni replied.

The clock ticking in the room was creating tension. Kuril felt it in his blood that he had to serve justice to whoever came to steal the Teardrop of Alexandria, the jewel he was guarding alongside Yanni. While Yanni was feeling anxious, Kuril was awaiting the time for the calling card's threat.

"Shouldn't we have gotten the police involved?" Yanni asked.

"Mr. Dawson said he contacted the officials," Kuril told him. "Guess he fucking lied, huh?"

"If I have to go head-to-head with one of the world's best thieves, I'm pulling a gun and running out of here."

The clock was still ticking, like a clock should, but Kuril and Yanni were waiting for an explosion to destroy the wall, followed by the entrance of a giant man ready to kill them so there were no eyewitnesses to his thievery. Yanni started to snap to the melody of a song, which Kuril responded by tapping his foot loudly, having it echo through the spacious room to continue the beat.

"You like synth-pop?" Yanni asked, trying to keep himself calm.

"Can't say I do," Kuril answered, "but that song has a nice bassline at the chorus."

The two of them continued sitting in their chairs waiting for the calling card's sender to make their grand entrance. The night was growing old, yet the warning about a Rose invasion kept the two men on their toes.

"If we live tonight, wanna grab a beer?" Yanni offered.

"I'm not one for alcohol, but I'll still show if you want."

"You're not a drinker?"

"Do I look like one?"

"Fair."

The spacious room had long forgotten the melody that the two men were playing. The entire area was silent, until both of them heard footsteps.

"No way," Yanni whispered. "You'd think he'd make his first impression in a grandiose fashion."

Yanni slowly took out his pistol and took a deep gulp. His hands were slightly twitching, but he was confident that he was going to take on this mysterious man. It was rather ironic that a man with so much confidence was struggling to grip onto his handgun.

"Yanni," Kuril silently spoke, "I'm going to check."

"Don't die on me, we're still going for drinks after this."

Kuril slowly stepped toward the exit of the room that contained the Teardrop of Alexandria. He walked into the hallway that connected a room with billions of dollars worth of value and a different empty room.

"Bravo!"

Kuril immediately took a defensive stance and scanned his surroundings. Someone else was in this building besides the two personnel.

"Kuril!" Yanni ran out of the room tightly gripping his pistol.

A figure stepped into the light of the hallway. He looked like your ordinary man, but had a smug smirk across his face and a condescending, yet taunting look. Yanni was trembling, yet filled to the brim with determination, all while Kuril was boiling in his own hatred.

"My name is Fifteen, I'm a member of Rose!"

His outfit was a normal windbreaker and a white t-shirt, as if he was a grown man about to go on a jog in the summer. He was wearing khakis and his hair was straight, yet dyed red.

"You're here for the Teardrop of Alexandria, aren't you?" Yanni asked, aiming his pistol at him.

"That's not very friendly. Is that how you greet your mother?" he jested.

"Sorry, Fifteen, but this area is restricted. You're going to have to leave," Yanni spoke, "or I'll have to make you."

That shift of tone was not taking any effect on Fifteen, which was shown by his immediate response.

"That's very fair, but I don't intend on leaving without that jewel."

"I have full authority to shoot you right now."

Yanni's seriousness was at maximum while Kuril just stood next to him watching the scene. In secret, he was analyzing the nature of his opponent, knowing a fight was going to go down. In the matter of a split second, the gun in Yanni's hand was gone and Fifteen was still in the same spot, but in a different pose. It was a matter of utilizing his cloud, which looked like super speed.

"You can't shoot me if you don't have a gun," said the comical Fifteen.

"That cockiness will be your downfall," Kuril said with a smirk. "Mark all six words I just spoke."

"You're such an intimidating man."

Despite calling Kuril intimidating, Fifteen was smiling. Fifteen was confident he was going to take that jewel and that two people with guns weren't an issue for the skill of his cloud.

"I'll be taking that jewel now," Fifteen said, casually walking past the two men.

"Not on my watch."

Kuril's eyes averted to the entrance to the room, flinging his arm toward the door. His arm turned to water and created a strand of water going to the door. The strand of water stretched itself out and covered the entire slot of the door.

"Water." Fifteen let out a laugh. "I'm so scared! Nice to see that you have a cloud."

He zoomed straight past the water, getting himself wet during his super speed showoff.

"One of you, what's the password to unlock the safe?"

"You'll have to kill me first," Yanni said, smiling and taking a glance at Kuril.

Kuril exchanged his smirk back, then went toward Fifteen. The two of them stood across from each other in the room. Fifteen turned around and faced Kuril, expecting a password from him. At this point, Kuril's water barrier was removed, but Fifteen was still wet. Kuril flung his hand, a dot of water touching the ground below him.

Kuril walked forward a bit, then dashed straight at Fifteen before turning to water. Fifteen just chuckled, but was met with a hand in his hair. On Fifteen's back was Kuril, who just regenerated out of thin air.

"You bastard! How the fuck did you just do that?" Fifteen yelled.

"Yanni! Get the pistol!"

Yanni was looking on from the hallway, but heard and saw Kuril's actions in the other room through the open door. Yanni took a look around and found his pistol on the ground and immediately picked it up.

"Kuril, I can't aim! He's going to speed right past the bullet!"

"Get off me, you fucking runt!"

Fifteen was struggling to take Kuril off of him, and at this point, Kuril was thinking of his next move. Kuril was still on top of Fifteen like he was being given a piggyback ride, gripping onto his hair.

"Yanni, toss me the pistol!" Kuril commanded using all the air in his lungs.

Yanni threw the pistol across the room, and both Fifteen and Kuril went to grab it, but Kuril smacked it out of the air and had it spin back to the door.

"Kuril!" Yanni screamed, knowing that Fifteen getting a pistol would be the end of them.

Kuril liquified yet again and disappeared, reappearing in front of the pistol and grabbing it. Kuril threw the gun in the air directly above him. The gun spun in the air toward the roof of the room, but only peaked a foot below the ceiling. The gun, such a deciding factor in this battle, showed that even with clouds, guns were still extremely useful in battle.

With no backup plan, Fifteen rushed toward Kuril using his speed, but Kuril already became water again. Fifteen scanned his sights, only to find nothing. Yanni was watching on by the entrance, astonished by the performance that was ongoing. Reappearing in the same piggyback position on Fifteen, he caught his own gun and aimed it to Fifteen's head.

Fifteen stood still. He was in complete shock at how easily defeated he was.

"You must read your opponent before you fight them," Kuril said, "that's how you win."

"I have no intention of submitting to you."

"Tell me who you are and who your coworkers are," Kuril demanded, "or I'll end your pathetic life right now."

"I work for Rose, I'm Fifteen."

"Who are the other members?" spoke Kuril, still on Fifteen's shoulders with the gun to his head.

"I refuse to speak."

"You know what that means?"

"I refuse to beg for my life."

"You won't need to." Kuril had already made up his mind even if he complied. "Now die and repent for your sins in hell."

"Fuck you."

The gun went off, Fifteen's body fell to the floor, and Kuril hit the ground alongside him. Brain matter was all over the floor, leaving a mess in the area where the jewel was supposed to be secured. Kuril immediately stood up right after taking the fall with Fifteen.

"Kuril, how?" Yanni started jumping up and down.

"It's my cloud," Kuril confirmed, "I can become water at will or make any part of my body water."

"No, but how did you teleport?"

"A fool thinks he knows his opponent, a tactician keeps learning about their opponent."

"Kuril, I'm serious. What the hell did you do back there?"

"My ability allows me to regain my human build at any point of water that I've generated. I used that drop on the floor near the gun to regenerate before he could notice and run over. The water disintegrates when I reform my body, but if you noticed, he was wet. I used the back of my hand's skin to keep his hair wet so I could rebuild my body on top of him."

"What?"

Kuril shook his hand and a droplet of water across the room.

"Watch," Kuril instructed.

Kuril's body became entirely water, and he became human again in the corner of the room, where there was a single droplet of water. The body of water where he dispersed into liquid had faded away.

"I can become whole again wherever there is water, but only the water I produced from my own cloud, which is my body."

"Why do your clothes come with you and not get wet?"

"Clouds have a property that adapts to their user, meaning that my clothes stick with my ability due to my will for such. I can also manipulate the water to my will as long as it's connected to my body."

"I see," Yanni said, smiling, "you're going to become so famous for what just went down."

"Not really," Kuril replied, "I don't intend on interviews and I'd like for it to remain private. You can take credit, but they'll probably target you."

"Yikes."

Kuril's clothes were already dark, so the stains weren't very easy to notice. The two men returned to their chairs with the corpse on the ground. Yanni was still gleeful while Kuril had grown exhausted.

"Wouldn't it be badass if we did that song again?" Yanni laughed.

And so, Yanni snapped. Kuril caught on with the snapping, and they were performing a synth-pop piece with their fingers and feet. The only difference in this performance from the last one was the body on the ground and the blood around it.

"How many more hours?" Kuril asked.

"About three more hours of watching then we can head out." Yanni checked his phone. "I should contact Junil."

"Why would you contact him?"

"He's the only non-corrupt official in this area and we just killed one of the Rose members, we're gonna need him on this case."

"I don't want to meet him," Kuril admitted, "there's something off about him."

"No way," Yanni said, "you don't want to meet the world's best detective?"

"His name."

"His name?"

"It's similar to mine." Kuril starred at Yanni. "Doesn't that mean something?"

"Dude, you're bugging out right now," Yanni replied, "I already sent a text."

"I don't want him here."

"It's too late. What's the issue anyways?"

Kuril grunted. "Fine."

And so time went on and the clock still ticked, just with a body in the room this time. Both the men were growing tired as their night shift of defending the Teardrop of Alexandria was nearing the end. It grew silent, but the amount of yawns grew exponentially. Yanni eventually stood up from his chair and started to pace around.

"Getting antsy?" Kuril asked, eyes looking as soulless as can be.

"I'm trying to not fall asleep."

"Those drinks," Kuril said, letting out a yawn, "tomorrow."

"Definitely. I'd fall asleep before we even reached the bar."

The exit opened again and the two men were back on alert. Their determination for their job was always to be met with high standard surveillance, no matter how tired they were. The footsteps started to echo even louder as Yanni gripped his pistol even tighter.

"Yours truly has arrived on the scene!"

The voice was one Kuril didn't recognize, but Yanni loosened his grip and let out a sigh of relief. His serious face turned to a casual smile as he approached the footsteps. The figure of the voice walked into the room and flung his arms open.

"Yanni!"

"Junil." Yanni let out a chuckle. "There's a dead man in front of your feet."

Junil jumped back a bit with the realization the dead body was right in front of the door. He slowly walked across it, trying to not step in the blood.

"You're quite clumsy for a detective," Kuril said, looking Junil dead in the eyes.

"He was shot in the back of his head from a 15° angle, going down from the right side to the left," Junil stated, surprising the blond man in front of him, "and as a result, obviously died."

"How can you determine that?"

"He was shot with the pistol to his head," Junil continued,

smiling with his attempt to crush Kuril's assumption, "it's likely one of you was somewhat above him, judging by the fact that you're all the same height or similar. Hard to tell from here."

"Color me surprised," Kuril admitted, "you are quite the detective."

"Quite the clumsy one?"

"I'm not taking back my statement, Mr. Junil."

"Stubborn," Junil said, laughing. "What's your name?"

"Kuril."

And with such a bold answer, the world around all three men froze. Yanni had no idea why the two men were suddenly combating each other with looks and looks only, but he had a hint that it had to do with Kuril's name.

"No one survived the massacre of the Violette," Junil pointed out, eyes staring into the soul of Kuril, "except one person."

"That was me," Kuril declared, "but who the fuck are you? Why do you have a Violet name?"

"I'm half Violet," Junil answered, "my father was Violet."

"Your mother?"

"She was from this city, where I was born and raised."

"I apologize for my rude behavior." Kuril put his hands in his pockets and tilted his head away. "If I'm the last living Violet, that means your father is dead."

"I'm an orphan." Junil's face didn't move an inch. "I grew up in an orphanage before being taken in by a wealthy family, where they used my intuitive excellence to sharpen my detective skills."

"So you were a detective your entire life?"

"Not necessarily," Junil added, "I was raised to become one once they took me in."

"Interesting."

Yanni listened in on the conversation, just a foot or two away from the two conversing men. He was confused, but wanted to pursue the answer to his sole question.

"What exactly do you mean by massacre?" Yanni asked.

"There was a village called Violette somewhere in the wild." Junil's head was tilted, almost to hide his expression. "Eleven years ago, Rose slaughtered every last one of them."

"I'm still here," Kuril pointed out, as if it weren't obvious.

"Why would they just slaughter a village of innocent people?" Yanni pursued.

"The Violet had a method of being able to confirm if someone was lying or not through just touching them," Junil went on, "and it was written in a scroll."

"So?"

"They refused to give the scroll, and as a result, they all…"

Kuril's expression was that of a man who had lost everything besides his will to keep fighting. Junil's notice of that made him fade his answer and send an expression to Yanni that it was a sensitive topic.

"I'm going to kill them."

Junil and Yanni looked at Kuril, not shocked at his lust for revenge, but surprised at his confidence.

"Kuril, you killed one of their members in a solid few minutes," Yanni spoke, "but you can't defeat all the other fourteen members."

"I'll help." Junil grinned. "I want them dead just as much as you do."

"I don't want your help," Kuril refused, "you'll only drag me down."

"Fair enough, but you should consider."

Junil escorted the men out during their shift and contacted the police to restrict the area for his own private investigation, which was already as far as he needed it to be. As the sun came up on the beautiful city of Velindas, the two men parted ways. Kuril headed to the motel where he was staying on the corner of the business side of the city. The city streets were not so filled that night, but the loud partying of the other side echoed throughout the working, tired streets.

Kuril opened the door to his low-grade motel room, which contained two beds, one of which was unused. The bed softened on Kuril's back as he groaned. He kicked his shoes off and dozed away in his blood-stained suit. Kuril's bed felt like heaven, but with the everlasting thoughts of revenge filling his mind, his world was hell. There was no doubt in Kuril's mind that all of Rose was going to crumble beneath him.

CHAPTER 11

"**F**or the love of God, can we stop robbing places and going to the Velindas alleyways?" a tall, pale man with dark hair asked.

"Do we have to complain?"

"At least do it elsewhere." The first man groaned. "The business parts are fuckin' rough."

"That's true." The second man sat down in the dirty alleyway. "But we don't need to complain."

"Aren't you the head of Rose?" the first man started up.

"Aren't you also the head of Rose, Two?"

"You're One," Two went on, "you control where we rob and when."

"Sit down next to me." One rested his eyes. "Let's take a breath."

Two decided to sit down next to One and rest his eyes alongside him. The peaceful quietness of the city at 4 a.m. was relaxing, as you couldn't hear the party people from the alleyways.

One was a tall, sort of pale man. His hair was fluffy in the front and black. He wore a nice dark purple jacket that hung to the middle of his thighs, but his arms could fit through the sleeves without there being extra length. He wore a white tee under that purple jacket accompanied by pitch black dress pants. His eyes were as black as his hair and could change the mood of the room he was in with one look.

Two on the other hand was tan and an inch and a half taller than One. His hair was also fluffy, but didn't have it grown out in the back as much as One. In contrast to One, his hair was also dyed white. Two wore glasses as well, but didn't strike as the nerd type. In fact, his glasses had red tinted lenses. He was more buff than One, but still wasn't a bodybuilder archetype. Two wore a brown jacket with a white shirt underneath and some normal slacks for pants.

As the two men were sitting down, just relaxing peacefully next to each other, light tapping was approaching One, who was closer to the depths of the alleyway.

"You hear that?" Two asked.

"It seems like a small animal."

A black cat slowly came out of the shadows and approached One. The cat had yellow eyes and fit the exact standard of a witch's cat. The feline's paws took a pause about a few feet away from One.

"Come on, little kitty. It's okay, I won't hurt you." One smiled.

The cat stood still, staring at One's face, almost as if it were slowly accepting his smile as a warm welcome. The cat slowly continued toward One, eventually reaching him in a matter of a few seconds. One's legs folded up in a criss-cross form and allowed the furball to jump into his lap, where it found comfort quickly.

"No way," Two said, letting out a laugh, "this man of all people is a cat person?"

"Kaylin and I fed a stray when we were kids." One stroked the cat's fur. "The cat kept coming to us, and as a result I learned how to be friendly with cats."

"Adorable." Two chuckled. "Kaylin being a cat person doesn't strike me as a surprise, though."

"She's sweet." One's eyes glowed. "She's my entire world."

"How do you love your sister that much?" Adam closed his eyes again.

"You never had siblings," One pointed out, "you wouldn't understand."

"No one I know with siblings is that addicted to them," Two mentioned, "you're just unordinary."

"I can't control it."

"Sounds like my best friend is a creep."

"Cut it out."

Silence filled the alleyway again as One closed his eyes. The cat was being stroked by One, who seemed to have his soft spot for felines. The world around them was silent, but the two of them felt each other in that moment.

"It's been a long time since we met," Two said, breaking the silence, "been through a lot."

One was trying to put his head down in the instance that Two opened his eyes, hoping Two wouldn't notice his watery eyes. As Two awaited a response, he opened his eyes to check on One, but took notice to his teary face.

"James, what's wrong?" Two was a mixture of confused and concerned, but was trying to grasp the situation cleanly.

"I love her so much, Adam," James started, "Kaylin is my whole world."

"I understand that, but why cry over it?" Adam asked.

"She was born into a world that won't give her what she needs to survive. She's blind, not physically able to defend herself, and her cloud has no fighting ability. The world won't give her a fighting chance."

"You love her that much?"

"She's all I have now, and I have to protect her."

"James." Adam was looking toward the outside of the alleyway. "You're a good guy."

"I never wanted to become a criminal."

"It's not your fault."

"Kaylin hates me, doesn't she?"

"She just doesn't want you to be a criminal." Adam was clearly tired of James' self-deprecating behavior. "She thinks it's wrong."

"Why won't she understand it's all for the Blooming Day?"

"She doesn't know what the Blooming Day is"—Adam closed his eyes again and leaned his head back against the wall—"only that it exists."

"Fifteen died yesterday," James mentioned, "the Blooming Day plan is in action."

"Do you really think this is how we should go about things?"

"It's for Kaylin."

Adam sighed. "Sure it is."

The alleyway became silent again, with few passerbys in the streets not caring about the two men sitting against the wall.

"We should get going." Adam stood up and stretched his muscles casually.

"Adam"—James got up alongside him—"I want to see her right now."

"She'll be back at the normal spot."

"I want to see her right now."

"Then let's go." Adam started walking out of the alleyway. "This is sad to watch."

"Alright."

Kuril was in for a stroll during the day, taking his time around the primary shopping district of Velindas and checking out new things. In the heat of the day, he was wearing a white tee and black basketball shorts, with normal black sneakers on. It wasn't exactly fancy, but in such temperatures, it let him breathe. He passed by a cat coffee shop with a television inside of it broadcasting the news. Intrigued, Kuril entered the shop to see what was on the news at the moment.

"Now that Fifteen is down, what will Rose do?" The news reporter added a hint of suspense to try and thrill up the situation.

Kuril wasn't surprised that the news was filled with Fifteen's death and that the reporters were using it as a tool to keep their viewers' eyes glued to the screen. He wondered if Junil kept the anonymity of the situation in his hand so Kuril wouldn't be targeted.

"Excuse me, sir," the waitress spoke, "you need to order if you want to stay here."

"I apologize. Get me anything," Kuril requested, "under 15 dollars."

"What do you actually want?"

"Surprise me."

"Sir, please just order something off the menu."

"I want a surprise." Kuril folded his arms.

"Coming right up," the waitress said, sighing.

During Kuril's wait for his surprise drink, a white-haired man approached his table. He took a seat directly across from Kuril, choosing the exact same table.

"This is my table." Kuril's expression changed.

"I'm not a Rose member."

"What?"

"You're correct." The man let out a laugh. "I am reading your mind."

Kuril sat there in shock. He had asked himself if the man across from him was a Rose member, then after the answer, he wondered if the man was in fact reading his mind.

"Who are you?"

"Fourteen, the one who's going to end your life for what you did to Fifteen."

"It would be cooler if you guys had names."

"We threw away our names for the sake of Rose," Fourteen

said, moving his hair across his head, which was blocking his eyes for half the conversation.

"Can I get my final drink before you end my life?"

"You don't insist on giving in."

"You can read my mind, huh?"

"It's my ability." Fourteen's face was filled with a giant smirk. "I'm gonna utilize it in a fight."

"A fight with me?"

"Of course."

The waitress placed a medium-sized, green drink on the table. "Your drink."

"Thank you." Kuril smiled and then took a sip.

"It's minty, huh?" Fourteen let out a chuckle.

"Stop reading my mind, it's creepy," Kuril demanded.

"I'll do what I wish."

"I'll beat your ass."

"For the sake of the Violet?"

"Where did you find me?"

"I searched for Fifteen's killer around these parts for a long time," Fourteen answered, "it's been about two days and I read your mind when you were focused on the news broadcast, and bang!"

"How many people did you search the minds of?"

"A shit ton."

Kuril took the final sip of the drink, left a twenty dollar bill on the table, then took his leave. Fourteen followed behind him. By height to height comparison, Fourteen was about two to three inches shorter than Kuril and looked about his age, which was 21 years old.

"Where are we fighting?" Fourteen's footsteps were right behind Kuril's.

"I'm thinking the flat desert would be a good fighting spot." Kuril answered.

"Sure!"

The two walked toward the outskirts of the city, eventually

approaching less and less street lamps to symbolize the end of the Velindas. The sun was beginning to set and the sweat was rolling down Kuril's face.

"Not used to the heat?" Fourteen asked.

"Violette was a village somewhere tropical, but I was never very fond of the high temperatures."

"I see."

The two continued down their path, with Kuril still in front. Kuril was strategizing on how to beat Fourteen during the walk to the plain desert, but he left with the same conclusion for each plan: Fourteen read his actions before they were performed. He had practically walked into a death trap.

"I think your plans are solid," Fourteen admitted, "Fifteen didn't lose to just anybody."

"Stop with the act."

"I'm serious." Fourteen went to Kuril's side. "Fifteen may have been arrogant, but he was smart. You aren't just anybody, Mr. Kuril. You're a real solid tactician."

"I don't want your compliments."

"I understand."

As they walked past the last street light, there was nothing except darkness ahead. Fourteen paused in his tracks and took out a pistol with suppression on it.

"This is where it ends for you, Mr. Kuril."

"I should've guessed." Kuril turned around, trying to strategize to save himself in such a dire situation.

"Do you think God exists?"

"God abandoned the Violet." Kuril looked Fourteen dead in the eyes. "If he exists, I'll kill him."

"You have quite the short temper."

"God started this war."

"So you believe in him?"

"I believe in the idea that I'll get my revenge on him."

Fourteen started to laugh. "That's quite interesting."

"If you die here, I may forgive him."

Fourteen's face changed expression, going from gleeful to serious. Kuril's face remained the same, a serious face with a mind that's running faster than it ever has.

"Stakes are high, I see it in your mind," Fourteen mentioned.

"I'm not dying."

"That confidence can go to your grave." Fourteen smiled again, raising his pistol, ready to end Kuril's short life.

"I'm not dying."

"I doubt it." Fourteen's smile grew larger, almost creepy. "To Hell you go with the rest of your people."

Kuril's eyes showed intense rage at that moment. Liquifying his arm, he flung himself toward Fourteen. In his life, taking insults was never hard, but after the people of Violette were slaughtered, he grew a short temper regarding comments on his own kind. Ready to leap at Fourteen and take action, he was met with a surprise, but not one from God.

"My, oh my!" a familiar voice spoke up from the street light, causing Kuril to pause in his tracks.

Fourteen and Kuril looked over at the voice, spotting a long brown-haired man in a trench coat. It was none other than the famed detective that roamed Velindas looking for action. Junil walked up to the two and lightly pressed on both their arms, causing both of them to put their arms back to their sides.

"You must be a Rose member, right?" Junil asked the shorter man.

"And you must be Junil."

"I had someone follow both of you, but I can't exactly tell what your ability is."

Fourteen looked into Junil's eyes. "Your thoughts."

"That's right. So why don't you shoot Kuril?"

Fourteen was frozen.

Junil smiled and closed his eyes. "Kill Kuril, Fourteen. Why don't you?"

"What the fuck?"

Kuril put his arm up to signal that he still existed. "What's happening?"

Fourteen was speechless.

The blond boy was being ignored to such an extent that he started tapping his foot and humming. He had no clue what Junil was thinking about and why Fourteen was so startled by those thoughts.

"So you know Two?"

"I know him very well."

Fourteen's eyes widened. "Why would he prioritize the enemy over me?"

Kuril caught Fourteen off guard and grabbed his gun as he was focused on Junil. Bending Fourteen's arm behind his back and pinning him to the ground, Kuril let out a sigh of relief.

"That works," Junil said, looking down at Fourteen.

"Seems like he can't read two minds at once." Kuril pointed the gun at Fourteen's head.

"Seems like you're the clumsy one." Junil chuckled.

Kuril nonchalantly fired into Fourteen's head.

"I offered you my help." Junil looked down at Kuril, who was still pinning down the dead body. "Next time you might not be so lucky."

"I was just careless."

"He wasn't a fighter, he was an informant."

"I was just careless," Kuril repeated, "don't make me say it again."

"Kuril, take my help."

"I don't like the police."

"I'm a private detective, I do my own work." Junil stared at him directly in his eyes. "I need someone like you to combine with my intuitive abilities."

"Why would you need me?"

"We're equal on power level, that much I have determined,"

Junil pointed out. "My intuition as a detective and your skills as a tactician will prove deadly for Rose."

"How can I trust you?" Kuril stood up.

"You just have to."

"Where did you find me?"

"I followed you and Fourteen from the shopping district. I kept myself cloaked behind buildings and wore a beanie to hide my hair."

"Let's go back to the motel I'm staying at." Kuril closed his eyes and sighed. "We'll discuss details there."

"Glad to be on the operation," Junil said, smiling, "but it only gets harder."

"I know that."

"Then let's be on our way."

The white tee wasn't stained with blood. Kuril walked alongside Junil, both men not calling for rides to enjoy the moment. The road back was much more calm for Kuril, and Junil was relieved to know that.

"What's going to happen to Fourteen's body?"

"I left my assistant to deal with it."

"You didn't call anyone," Kuril pointed out, "how did he know you were there?"

"You have a good memory." Junil placed his hands in his pockets. "I had a hand signal to bring him in. I had him start following me when I started to follow you."

"Clever."

"You're really calm in high-pressure situations, Kuril."

"If you show frustration, the opponent will press harder to break you."

"I was sarcastic. You play chess I suppose?"

"I'll get a round in with you soon."

"That's great."

The shopping district was louder as they approached it, with radios booming and groups of teenagers laughing and strolling along without a care in the world. The city was glowing with another night full of shenanigans, but the two young men knew something the people didn't: another member of Rose took a fall.

"Junil, take that beanie off. You look stupid."

"I can't." Junil averted his eyes to Kuril then toward the opposite side to scan the scene. "I'm a celebrity here."

"That surprises me."

"Shut up."

Sooner than later, word went around regarding the passing of Fourteen. Rose caught on quickly, which called for the urgency of a meeting with two of the fifteen members murdered. With no leads, the petals of Rose decided to put their heads together for their collective safety.

"Another meeting for Rose," Adam said, giving out a sigh, clearly not interested in the affairs.

"Why are we gathered here? Where is Fourteen?"

Thirteen people were gathered around in a circle, sitting on chairs. They analyzed each other's looks to see who knew what was happening and who was as confused as them. All of them came to the same conclusion: only the top man knew what this meeting was for.

"You think One is finally gonna tell us his name?" a man asked the person sitting next to him.

"Only Kaylin and Two know his name and they won't budge, I doubt he would too," responded the other member.

"Alright, settle down," James spoke up, "I have an announcement."

"Fourteen isn't here yet," a normal-looking man in a suit and tie mentioned, "you're going to conduct this meeting without him?"

"Fourteen is dead, Eleven." James' expression didn't change, almost as if he never cared.

"Sounds like someone is out to get us," a brunette young lady with short hair and bangs said, bringing things to a faster pace.

"You think the police are doing their job?" Eleven asked.

"What the hell? Mourn the loss of your fellow comrade!" a booming voice yelled, but no one paid attention. There were more important matters to them: their lives.

"What I want to know is why Thirteen is so sure someone is out to get us," a voice spoke, putting suspicion on their own member.

"Two members down in the matter of days." Thirteen looked down. "Someone wants us dead."

"A lot of people do," said Adam, who let out a laugh. He didn't care for the death of Fourteen at all.

"You're all disappointing me right now." Thirteen's words were louder than her voice, angering half the people in the meeting.

"How so?"

"First of all, Six, you haven't said a word about solving the issue." Thirteen was ready to bring up her proposal. "It seems only Eleven wants to look into this."

"I just think it's a threat to all of us," Eleven clarified. "If we can't break through our threats, are we really Rose?"

"I'll kill the mastermind behind the deaths of Fifteen and Fourteen." Thirteen's confidence made everyone in the room exchange looks.

"You'll end up like them," Six spoke again, trying to contrast the confidence. "How do we know you have a plan?"

"I don't, nor do I need one." Thirteen's eyes were on fire.

"Please let me go with you," a delicate girl Thirteen's age pleaded, "I don't want you to get hurt."

"Your cloud is prime defense, Twelve," Thirteen mentioned, "I could use it, but I don't want you to get hurt either."

"Are you saying you don't want to risk her getting hurt? She's in a gang, dumbass!" Six clenched his fists and his face grew more red over the protection and care the two showed for each other.

"She isn't coming with me and that's final." Thirteen's mind was made up from the start.

"I'm coming," Twelve insisted, only getting more desperate trying to assert herself.

Thirteen's expression shifted as her fist tightened and she turned toward her comrade. "I'll kill myself right here if you even think about coming with me."

"Hey, what the fuck!" Six shouted, getting up from his chair and walking over to Thirteen.

"Stop it, Six," Adam spoke, "that expresses her determination, not her will to die or live."

"She's threatening suicide!"

"She's trying to protect Twelve."

Six went back to his chair and sat down, crossing his arms.

"Where can I find them, One?" Thirteen asked.

"Fourteen died near the end of the city, by where the dune begins," James pointed out, "Seven, if you could run a scan on that general area to show who was at the scene at the time of his death, we could determine who killed him."

"Sure, I don't mind." Seven finally spoke his first words of the meeting. "I could head over right now."

"Meeting is disbanded," James declared, "Thirteen and Seven, go analyze the scene where Fourteen died."

Everyone got up and scrambled out of the tiny abandoned building they met in. On their way out, Three, a tan man in a sharp blazer, who was one of the tallest in the gang, crossed paths with Twelve.

"You know," Three whispered, "you can't play the good girl forever."

"I'm not sure how long you can play the mysterious guy role either," she replied.

A sardonic smile took over Three's face as his eyes shut. "It's adorable to think you have a chance against me."

"Isn't it convenient that the meeting ended? I wonder why One ended it so abruptly."

"Oh? What ever could you be getting at?"

"I'm onto all three of you. Don't think you'll get away with this."

Listening in, Thirteen stopped moving along the crowd to

try and understand what Twelve and Three were talking about. It seemed as if they both had eyes on each other as if they were enemies. Worried for Twelve, Thirteen tried to piece together what the two were talking about, but couldn't reach a conclusion.

Seven interrupted Thirteen's train of thought. "Let's be on our way, Thirteenerino!"

"Yeah." Thirteen drew a blank as she continued looking on at Twelve and Three, who were starting to go their own ways. "Let's go."

"Sweet!"

"And don't call me that."

Everyone had finally gone their separate directions, some going in groups and some going solo, but they split up nonetheless. Thirteen and Seven left the base of operations, which was an abandoned office building toward the opposite edge of the city from where Fourteen died, one that hasn't been touched in a long time. The two had to walk through the entire city to reach the scene where Fourteen was killed, but they didn't mind.

"Hey, Thirteen, why do you care for Twelve so much?"

"Long story," Thirteen answered, "it'll bore you."

"Long walk," Seven replied. "I'm already bored, so tell me that story."

"Don't tell anyone," Thirteen demanded, "or I'll kill you."

"I'm not really scared of threats, but I'm not going to tell anyone regardless."

"No one else knows this besides One and Twelve, but I come from Violette, the village we took down. I left that home a long time ago because I felt neglected and I was continuously bullied by peers."

"Didn't you recommend we raid the village?" Seven asked, walking next to Thirteen with his hands in his pockets.

"I didn't do it for the benefit of Rose, I did it because I wanted everyone there dead."

"That's brutal," Seven responded, "but what does this have to do with Twelve?"

"While we were raiding, I found the man I hated the most in that village. He was my age, a relentless child when it came to making me feel awful."

"Go on."

"Twelve used her cloud to protect him." Thirteen's brown eyes became empty, yet aggressive—the highest layer of malice Seven has seen yet.

"So why do you like her?"

"After the raid ended, I had a one-on-one talk with her about it." Thirteen's face cooled down. "She apologized, but didn't agree with me. She thought that no matter what, everyone deserves a second chance."

"I've never seen her hurt anything before," Seven mentioned. "She's sweet."

"I grew interested in her thought process, and eventually grew closer to her as I studied her."

"So you're good friends?"

"We're a lot more than good friends." Thirteen's expression wasn't changing at this point on, but she did slightly avert her head away from Seven.

"Are you kidding me?" Seven turned to Thirteen to try and read her expression.

"No."

"A Rose love story." Seven said, following with a laugh. "Isn't that adorable?"

"You see why I don't want her getting involved in these affairs?"

"Of course."

The two Rose members continued on their walk, knowing it was going to be a lot longer than that story. On the occasion, Seven would attempt small talk or mention the news, sometimes even putting speculations for Fourteen's death on the table. Despite all the attempts, Thirteen wasn't very interested.

"You aren't quite the talker." Seven stuck out his tongue.

"Why didn't we take a cab?"

"Good question, and I have no idea."

Eventually, the two reached their finish line: the scene of Fourteen's death. It was surprisingly empty. His location of death was kept private by police, but there were no investigators nearby. It had only been a day since he died, yet no one seemed to care.

"Why is it empty?" Thirteen asked.

"Junil left the case to his assistant," Seven answered, "or so the news said."

"So it was a lone case?"

"Junil didn't let the police in on it."

"That's odd."

Seven's index finger on his right hand started to glow. "Stay back a little."

Thirteen moved back to about thirty yards from the crime scene. Seven's finger touched the pavement, followed by him moving in a circle, keeping his finger on the ground. His finger left a trace of a glowing substance, which was from his cloud. Seven's cloud held the ability to read all information he wanted in a specific area, which would be defined by the circle he created. His cloud also held the ability to rewind time in his ring, but was limited to small spaces and time. After finishing the circle, Seven moved back to Thirteen.

"Ready to see who killed him?" Seven asked.

"Show me."

The glowing substance remained, but as Seven watched on, he confirmed the facts of the situation. It was simple to him at this point: three people involved, one of them died.

"Some blond guy." Seven pieced together the crime scene. "He was with Junil."

"Is it true he was just shot so easily?"

"No." Seven glanced toward Thirteen. "He was distracted by the detective."

"Distracted by what?"

"He was trying to kill a different man." Seven's confident tone convinced Thirteen. "Because that man killed Fifteen."

"So we have two targets?"

"You're correct."

"What was the other man's name? Where can we find him?"

"I have no idea where we can find him, but his name is Kuril."

Thirteen's face stiffened up. The aura she gave off caused Thirteen to feel a weight on his body. There was clear bloodlust in her eyes. She was no longer playing a simple game of life, she was now on a journey to end the life of Kuril. She looked at her hand, which was twitching from all the chemical reactions in her brain. There was one thing certain in her mind through all that confusion: Kuril had to die.

"Thirteen, are you okay?"

"I'm going to kill Kuril." Thirteen's focus was on Seven, intimidating him unintentionally. "That is the man Twelve saved."

"You're saying a Violet is trying to get revenge?"

"I'm going to kill him."

"First, we have to report this to all of Rose."

"He is going to die," replied Thirteen.

"Definitely."

The area was filled with silence, but after thirty seconds, Thirteen walked away. Seven followed her.

"Rest easy, Fourteen." Seven looked back at the spot Fourteen died in. "We'll avenge you."

CHAPTER III

"Good morning, Kuril." Junil took a sip from his coffee on the motel bed.

"Why are you staying here?" Kuril asked.

"They probably got leads on me. It's safer if I'm underground at a dusty motel."

"You don't get protection?"

"It's a long story, but yes I don't have protection." Junil held the mug away from his face to not let the steam get to his face.

"Guessing by the order we're going in, next up is Thirteen."

"We don't have a specific order, it's just sheer coincidence we've been following one."

"Spot and kill?"

"You make it sound cruel."

The door knocked, interrupting Junil's relaxing morning coffee. He slowly placed the mug on the table, getting up slowly, glancing at Kuril. Kuril nodded, so Junil slowly walked toward the door. Taking a look through the peephole, he noticed a girl with a delicate physique. Junil slowly opened the door, and without asking, the girl walked in.

"Who are you?" Junil asked.

The girl didn't respond, but instead, enclosed herself within a pink substance that fit her body perfectly. To anyone else, it just looked like she received a pink overlay, but there was clearly a meaning to her action. The pink substance came out of thin air and she didn't even move to apply it across her body. In fact, it was almost like she was trapped in a piece of gum that she could flexibly move in.

"I'm sorry, but who are you?" Junil asked again, ready to take action.

"Oh, sorry, I'm Twelve."

The two men exchanged glances, both shocked that their location was so easily found out. Twelve was at ease and even smiled to show she wasn't going to hurt them.

"It's okay." Twelve's smile filled the room. "I'm friendly."

"What do you want? How did you find us?" Kuril was finally getting out of bed.

"All of Rose knows you are the two men responsible for the two deaths recently," Twelve answered.

"How did you find us?" Kuril repeated.

"I'm the only one who knows you're both here." Twelve put the tension to a close. "Seven's sketch of what you two looked like reminded me that I saw those two exact men come here."

"Isn't that one hell of a coincidence?" Junil was getting suspicious.

"You'll just have to trust me."

"What exactly do you want?" Kuril asked, taking the tide into his favor by speeding up the conversation.

"I want to talk privately"—Twelve walked farther into the motel room—"a private location of your choice is fine."

"How can you trust us?"

"How can you make progress without trust?"

Junil and Kuril looked at each other, both confirming that

they should have a discussion with Twelve in order to proceed with their mission to end Rose's operations.

"Why can't we talk here?" Kuril's questions kept coming, but it didn't bother Twelve.

"I don't think this area is very private," Twelve looked toward the bathroom, "didn't this motel have a scandal of recording girls showering with secret cameras before?"

"It was a long time ago." Kuril let out a sigh. "So another spot?"

"I'd like that."

"There's an abandoned church nearby." Kuril shook his head to clear the hair away from his eyes.

Twelve chuckled. "I like the bedhead."

Kuril chose not to respond.

"For our security, we can't let you leave our sight until our business is finished." Junil put the pressure back up.

"That's fine." Twelve attempted to ease the pressure back down just as it rose.

"Should we be on our way?" Kuril asked.

"Let's go," Twelve said, smiling, "and thank you for cooperation. You two are paranoid, but sweet souls."

"It's not an issue." Junil smiled back.

Kuril got up and walked toward the exit of the room without a word. He was followed by the two into the Velindas sunlight. The three of them walked through the motel exit, all in their own peaceful and relaxed stride. Despite that, Kuril and Junil held one coherent thought: what does this private conversation hold for them?

"Before we reach our spot." Twelve paused the walk. "I ask this very seriously: do you trust me?"

"I'm putting my trust in you," Junil confirmed.

Kuril didn't respond, but Twelve took Junil's answer to heart and they went on their way. Eventually reaching the abandoned church, the three entered through the ruined doors. They closed the doors behind them.

The church was shining with light through the stained glass. What was once a place of worship transformed into a ground of ruins. Velindas never got rid of the church, but the city council had plans to revitalize it due to the religious importance it held for the city before it was abandoned. The church was forsaken due to an initial raid and slaughter in the building by a gang long ago. Those in charge of the raid were sentenced to death, and the church closed as a moment of silence. That "moment of silence" never ended, and as a result, the church was put away to the side. It was never in the way of Velindas, so it remained on the premises of the city as a sight to memorialize those who lost their lives that day.

Kuril grabbed a creaky chair and placed it in the middle of the church. Rather than grabbing a seat, Junil sat on the edge of a church pew that was horizontally across from Kuril. Twelve walked over in front of the two men. Out of nowhere, she put her hand out and became enclosed in a pink, translucent half-sphere. The half-sphere was similar to a spherical cap, in which the sphere stopped when it touched the ground. Twelve was entirely covered in this pink sphere, which almost resembled a bubble.

"The meaning of this?" Junil crossed his arms and put his right leg over his left.

"It's just protection," replied Twelve, "my cloud makes sure I'm safe as long as I'm enclosed in it."

"I see," Junil went on, "at least we can hear you loud and clear."

Kuril remained silent, as if he were thinking about something else and had no care for the situation at hand. In reality, he was thinking of the situation extensively.

"I've come to make peace," Twelve stated, "but I'd like to be heard out."

"My ears are open." Junil was ready to get the show on the roll.

"Mine aren't." Kuril's expression was the same, but the words spoken were said with such a tone that everyone in the church knew he didn't want to withdraw from this war.

"Please, just listen," Twelve pleaded.

"Everyone in Rose is going to rot in hell"—Kuril's eyes became fixated on Twelve, filled with the primal instinct to kill—"that includes you."

"You have to hear me out!" Twelve was basically begging for Kuril to listen.

"I don't want to."

"Kuril," Junil intervened, "listen."

Kuril's expression softened as he turned to Junil. Kuril's eye bags were visible, his face was cold, and his expression was that of a man who had lost his world. In truth, Kuril did lose everything: his friends, his family, his home. Kuril was a man who wanted nothing except the happiness of life, but that happiness was stripped of him after the people of his homeland were slaughtered.

"You monsters killed everyone I loved." Kuril looked back at Twelve. "Why should I spare you more time before you knock at the door of Satan's home?"

"What are you talking about?" Twelve asked.

"Were we that small to you? Tell me!" Kuril yelled, clenching his fists.

"I-I'm sorry, I have no idea what you're talking about." Twelve was slowly regaining her passive side yet again.

"Did you slaughter everyone I loved and just forget about it, leaving me with more scars than you could ever imagine?"

"He's talking about Violette." Junil turned into an acting mediator. "The village massacred by Rose."

"You're the last living Violet?" Twelve asked, grasping onto what little peace there was.

Kuril's eyes looked straight into Twelve's soul, giving her the answer she needed. He was the last living member of the Violet.

"You must have been through so much." Twelve's eyes were swelling with tears. "I'm so sorry for what Rose did to Violette and the people there."

"Your apology has no weight." Kuril's hand made a fist, but she was still safe in her own bubble.

"Tell me." Twelve looked straight into Kuril's eyes just as he did earlier. "Do you regret living?"

"I have to live, so the Violet can rest peacefully," Kuril responded, "I'm glad I survived."

"How long were you under that bed?"

Kuril's face loosened up, and the sudden realization hit him.

"You're the one who saved me?" Kuril's eyes were no longer hard to look at, but rather, they were filled with confusion and joy.

"If you were that kid, it seems like it."

"I'm not here for this fuckin' sob story." Junil scoffed. "I'm leaving."

"I'll handle matters from here, Junil."

Junil got up and left the church with such ease. It was almost surprising for him to leave the church so quickly and not care for the conversation. Nonetheless, the other two in the church dismissed it and went back to their conversation.

"I'm sorry for the way I acted." Kuril looked down, his facial expression barely visible to Twelve. "I thank you for letting me live."

"Please." Twelve started to plead again. "Stop killing. This isn't what your people would want."

"You don't know that." Kuril looked back up. "Only I do."

"Will you really not budge?"

"I won't."

"Then I ask one more thing." Twelve wasn't going to persist on the previous topic. "Could you at least spare Thirteen?"

"Why Thirteen?"

"I love her." Twelve was almost smiling. "She's my world. I couldn't live without her."

"Can I ask a question?"

"Go ahead."

"How many people did you kill in that massacre?" Kuril's question was more influential to the situation than Twelve could imagine.

"I didn't hurt anyone"—Twelve brushed her hand through her hair—"I'm not that type of person."

"I'll spare you both then."

"Thank you." A beatific expression filled the Rose member's face. What she really wanted was the safety of Thirteen.

"Any other matters?"

"Someone had something during that massacre," Twelve started, "it was like a necklace."

"What about a necklace?"

"It was gold and shaped like a Violet flower," Twelve explained, "it was simply beautiful."

"That was my teacher's necklace." Kuril's unblinking face kept staring into Twelve. "He taught me how to use my cloud as the heir to the village chief position."

"I didn't know it was his."

"It simply belongs to me now that he has passed." Kuril jumped to the chase. "Do you have it?"

Twelve reached into her pockets and grabbed the necklace. Taking it out made Kuril's heart skip a beat as it was something reminiscent of his past. It was the most beautiful necklace Kuril had ever seen.

Twelve let down her bubble to approach Kuril with the necklace. Kuril stood up, looking down at her face. She was a little short, but it didn't bother Kuril. In a speechless moment, Kuril's hand opened, and the necklace was placed in his palm. He closed his hand and placed the necklace in his pocket.

Kuril then hugged Twelve, which caught her by surprise.

"Thank you so much." Kuril was so hurt after many years and he never expected a Rose member to be the one he would thank for anything.

Twelve was silent, but wrapped her arms around Kuril. She slowly embraced the hug, smiling into his shoulder. The two held that position for ten seconds, before the silence was broken by a single gunshot.

In that unique moment, Kuril's short-lived happiness was cut short. Twelve fell limp, wrapped by Kuril's arms. She was no longer moving. Kuril was oddly not stained with blood, but he was left with a stain on his memory instead: the death of the one person he was grateful for. His arms loosened up, his eyes were in shock, his body was frozen with the occasional twitch. Kuril was looking for his words, but only found stutters.

Junil re-entered the church with a gun in his hand and a smirk on his face, "Wasn't that quite a nice shot?"

"Junil... why?" Kuril could only speak.

"That's three Rose members down," Junil said, "twelve left."

"Junil." Kuril found his words. "Get out."

"What?"

"I said get the fuck out!"

"I don't follow, Kuril."

"I'm..."

"Kuril, I killed her." Junil was still behind Kuril, standing at the church entrance. "I found a hole in the side of the building and—"

"Get the fuck out before I kill you!"

"You're saying you didn't want her dead?"

"Get out." Kuril was still in place. "Now!"

Junil put the pistol away and walked out of the church building. It was almost like the devil himself had killed an angel in church. Gracious as an angel, lovely as could be, Twelve was dead.

Kuril's inability to feel sadness was only met with his ability to feel anger. He was more than filled with rage. He was filled with endless despair within him, taking guilt for the death of Twelve. It was self-blame, distress, and anguish mixed into his own self-pity for the terrible life he had already lived. He could only look up to the church roof and plead to God for the strength to move. Kuril fell to the ground with Twelve still in his arms, slowly finding the strength to move. He stopped twitching, then placed her on the church floor, facing toward the heavens.

"The angels will take you." Kuril turned around as he tried

to avoid looking at Twelve. "There's a spot in heaven reserved for you."

The church was filled with silence yet again. Kuril, on the other hand, was filled with endless pain.

In the motel room, Junil sat on his bed, contemplating his choice. It wasn't Twelve's death that bothered him, but rather, how her death would impact the operation to eliminate Rose. Reaching into his pocket, he grabbed his phone and dialed a number. The phone rang for a few seconds before being answered, and Junil's mouth ran the second it was.

"Adam, I need your help." Junil laid on his bed, "I killed Twelve."

"What's wrong?"

"Kuril didn't want her dead," Junil answered, "apparently she saved his life."

"So why have I been called?"

"Adam." Junil needed help. "I don't know how to fix the bond between Kuril and I."

"First talk to him," Adam said, "then move from there."

"Adam." Junil tried to keep him interested.

"I'm busy."

Adam hung up the phone. Junil sat in silence from there on, constructing scenarios in his head. In truth, he had believed Kuril would never forgive him, and he accepted it. If that would be the case, he'd have to operate solo.

Adam and Junil were childhood friends and always stayed connected. It was ironic: a detective and a gang member always in contact working together. Adam's friendship was immeasurable to Junil, and Adam would do a lot for Junil. The two were inseparable.

The door flung open and in came Kuril. His face was that of a man who lost more than he could lose. There was endless despair in every part of him: his face, his eyes, his stride. Junil watched as Kuril dragged himself into bed. At this point it was the ending of the morning, but Kuril was too tired to keep moving. He wanted just an ounce of sleep so he could return to unconsciousness again. The day felt too long, almost never-ending to Kuril.

"I'm sorry." Junil broke the silence. "I thought I was supposed to kill her."

"Repent for your sins, Junil, but don't do it in front of me."

"What do you mean?"

Kuril flung his arm toward Junil from his bed, liquifying his entire left arm and submerging Junil's face in water. "Something was awfully suspicious when Fourteen said you knew Two."

Junil started to suffocate on the water. Placing his hand on the water that surrounded his head, the water instantly became gas as Junil coughed. "Let me speak before you try to kill me."

"What is your relation to Rose?"

"I'm only affiliated with Two."

"Why?"

"Childhood friends."

"That makes you affiliated with Rose."

Kuril liquified and immediately regained composition next Junil, grabbing his neck. Slithers of the skin on his hand liquified as the stream of water sent itself into Junil's nostrils to suffocate him. In retaliation, Junil reached for Kuril's head. As Junil tapped the temple of Kuril's head, the Violet fell limp to the floor, noting that Junil had stood up and he had lost control of his water.

"I'm your ally, Kuril. I am not affiliated with Rose. I'm on a mission to take them out."

Kuril stood up after ten seconds and punched Junil, who took the blow to his nose without retaliating. "You killed Twelve."

"You're allowed to take out your anger on me, but if it involves killing me, I can't let you do that." Junil held onto his nose. "You need to work with me to take out Rose. If you want to kill me, wait until we topple over their gang."

"You made a mistake, a grave one. Make things right." Kuril turned to his side, facing away from Junil. "Just respect her wish to keep Thirteen safe."

"How will we live if Thirteen attacks us?"

"We'll get there when we get there."

"Kuril, if there's anything I can do…"

"Help me destroy Rose." Kuril took up Junil's offer. "Kill all of the members besides Thirteen."

"I understand."

"I don't forgive you, and I probably never will," Kuril went on, "but I do need your help."

"Why aren't you mad anymore?"

"I don't care too much about her, but I'm still not happy you ended her life." Kuril hopped back on his bed and rolled over. "Let's just make things right and follow her will while going by ours."

"It's a good idea to dig into your brain," Junil agreed. "I'll fix what went wrong."

Junil looked out the window of the motel room, "Do you think we can really avoid killing Thirteen?"

"I'll kill her if we need to," Kuril admitted.

"They know what we look like and who we are now."

"Someone is probably out to get us." Kuril tossed himself across the bed and laid on his back. "I'm not worried."

"You're not really one who takes precautions," Junil noted. "That's odd for someone as wise as you."

"I do what I can in the moment, otherwise it just isn't my issue."

"Fair."

The two sat in silence. Junil was wondering about the next Rose member out to get them, but Kuril was in the middle of mourning. Though he was ready to move on if he needed to, he wanted to embrace every moment of his grief. To Kuril, this was a beautiful sadness, but to Junil, it was a symbol of regret.

"It's almost noon." Junil stood up and stretched. "Want to go for a walk?"

"You mean you want to go and spot Rose members?"

"You pick up hints quite easily."

"You didn't drop any difficult ones."

Kuril stood up and cracked his back. While stretching his arms, he stretched his legs. Laying down for just a moment does a lot to Kuril, who easily relaxes. Junil on the other hand can get comfortable quickly, but is constantly on alert for his job.

Without a word spoken between them, they both went out the door, ready to find Rose members and to eliminate them. In such a world, clouds can't be stopped. Those who have clouds are sentenced to death rather than jail due to the easy methods of escape. Therefore, killing someone with a cloud isn't frowned upon if it was a criminal or in self-defense. There is no need to apprehend those with clouds, they just die.

The sun hit the both of them right as they walked out of the motel. Junil reached into his pocket, pulled out a pair of sunglasses, and continued walking. Kuril wasn't bothered by the sun, but felt the incredible heat on his back. Following Junil's footsteps, Kuril kept an eye out for any members of Rose. Though they usually wandered the city without a care in the world, they were still wanted. What made them special, however, was the fact that they couldn't be identified. Rose members had no names and no pictures; the police had no intel on them whatsoever. Rose members walked free every single day because of that.

"Want to grab a bite?" Junil asked.

"Let's make it quick."

Junil and Kuril took a stop at a convenience store, where Junil took a party-sized bag of chips. He walked up to the cash register, scanned it himself, put five dollars down, and walked toward the exit. It was a simple process, but the cashier was not happy.

"You can't just do that," the cashier spoke. "Remember that next time."

"Sorry ma'am." Junil's apology was as fake as he wanted it to sound. "Maybe next time I'll switch it up."

"You better!"

Junil groaned and walked out of the building. He opened the bag of chips and dumped a handful into his mouth.

"Want some?" Junil asked.

"No thanks." Kuril declined the offer. "I'm not a fan of sour cream and onion."

"I see"—Junil took another handful of chips and dropped them into his mouth— "I don't see any Rose members."

"We aren't going to find some off the bat," Kuril explained, "they aren't just everywhere."

"I wish they were."

"No, you don't."

"My cloud could take any of them down," Junil bragged, "I'm a high-end fighter."

"I totally believe that." Kuril fixated his glare toward Junil.

"Yeah, and it's really nice being so strong."

"You better not overrate yourself." Kuril started looking at the street ahead. "Rose's boss is my prey."

"So be it."

The two kept walking, keeping an eye out for anyone who looked remotely suspicious. Judging by the fact that their identities were already known by Rose, they were waiting for an ambush. Their preparation wasn't very strong, but they were more confident they'd win any fight they would face.

A short girl with her eyes closed crashed into Kuril's shoulder. She lost her balance and hit the ground, and in a strange turn of events, struggled to get up. She had black hair that went down to a bit under her shoulders. It was straight hair, but stylized to be wavy. It was a look that matched her very well, especially when complimented with her entirely black outfit, consisting of a long skirt down to her knees and a sweater that looked a little too big on her. In fact, the neckline was somewhat bigger than you would expect and her arms could still fit through the sleeves, despite the little folds at the wrist that were visible.

In contrast to Kuril's black basketball shorts and white tee, it was a very good looking outfit. However, it didn't make much sense in Velindas, as the city was normally dry and hot. Junil's sandy-yellowish brown trench coat, almost a dark shade of beige, didn't match the climate of Velindas either. Despite wearing two contrasting colors, Kuril was the only one who really looked normal.

"Open your eyes, lady." Junil scoffed.

"I apologize." Kuril crouched down and grabbed her wrist, lifting her back up. "Are you alright?"

"I'm fine, thank you." she regained her balance. "But I need help."

"Is this the start of a pyramid scheme?" Junil asked.

"No, I'm actually lost."

"Lost?" Kuril was hinting for her to elaborate.

"I'm blind," the girl said. "My name is Kaylin."

"Nice to meet you, Kaylin." Kuril glanced at Junil then back at her. "Do you need help finding your guardian?"

"If you could please call them to pick me up," Kaylin begged, "I'd really appreciate it."

Kuril took out his phone, "What's the number?"

Kaylin read out the number from her memory in confidence, almost as if this situation has repeated itself several times. Kuril put the phone to his ear, and in a short amount of time, the number picked up.

"Hello? Is this the guardian of Kaylin?" Kuril asked.

"That's us," the man on the line responded, "can we pick her up?"

"Sure thing." Kuril looked around. "We're by Closedown Avenue."

"We're on the way."

The number hung up, and Kuril put his phone away.

"Your guardians are quite rude, aren't they?" Kuril joked.

"They're Rose members." Kaylin went along with it. "They aren't the most polite people."

Kuril and Junil turned to each other, both realizing what was awaiting them.

"They? Rose?" Junil pursued.

"There are two of them," Kaylin answered, "and they're Rose members."

"So who are you?"

"I'm the boss' sister."

"What number?"

"I'm not in the gang."

"Never killed anyone?"

"I'm clean." Kaylin was confused, "Why?"

"Well, shit."

Kuril and Junil were both thinking of ideas, and then Junil had one.

"Let's take her hostage," Junil whispered into Kuril's ear.

"That's kind of low, but alright," Kuril whispered back.

"Hm? Oh, they texted me," Kuril lied, "they said they'll pick you up at Kibbler Street."

"Then should we go?" Kaylin asked.

"Yeah, of course."

The three of them walked down the city, Kaylin holding Kuril's hand through the city as a form of guidance and Junil eating chips. The business side of the city was bustling, but it wasn't too bad for the trio. They were walking at a good pace, but Kaylin didn't know she was going to be brought to a motel room.

"Hey, you!" a voice boomed through the crowd in the street.

Junil and Kuril exchanged looks, trying to figure out who he was talking to.

"Are you talking to me?" Junil asked.

"Both of you!" The man walked over.

"I recognize that voice." Kaylin butted in on the conversation, "That's Ten, isn't it?"

"Kaylin." Ten was looking for words through his anger. "You're with Junil and Kuril!"

Ten was a man with green hair, almost lime. It was very clearly dyed, but he also had a perm as well. He was normal height, being around the same height as Kuril. He had good posture and wasn't very muscular, but definitely had some intimidation by his looks. He wore a normal band tee with black basketball shorts. It was a strange outfit, but not too questionable.

"The Rose murderers?"

"Yes!"

Kaylin let go of Kuril's hand and tried directing herself to Ten's voice.

"You people killed our members?" Kaylin was horrified.

"So what?" Kuril was starting to lose his temper.

"Why?"

"You fuckin' killed my entire village!"

Kaylin went silent and gripped onto Ten's arm, his eyes focused on Kuril. Junil walked to a trash can and threw out his bag of chips, which was already almost empty. He came back, licked his fingers, then dried them on his shirt.

"Give us the girl," Junil demanded, "now."

"Hell no!" Ten yelled.

"By force it is."

Junil's left hand glowed orange, then he charged at Ten. He grabbed Ten's head and suddenly Ten couldn't move.

"Grab Kaylin," Junil directed Kuril, "you have ten seconds!"

Kuril ran toward Kaylin, who tried to get away, but didn't make it very far. She struggled, but Kuril had her wrapped in his arms. He picked up Kaylin, who was struggling to even fight back, and started to run. Eventually, Ten regained control of his body and immediately charged after Kuril.

Junil followed after Ten. Kuril, following his own agenda, had a drop of water fall from his hand as he entered a dead end alleyway. Ten went toward the alleyway. Kuril lightly placed Kaylin in the alleyway and waited for Ten to walk into the alleyway, which was a part of his trap.

"I'm sorry, Kaylin, but I have to do this."

Kaylin was silent, and footsteps grew louder, echoing inside the alleyway. Ten was at the entrance, but before he could rush in, Kuril turned to water and reappeared right under him. With a full-force uppercut, Kuril made sure Ten hit the ground. Junil, who was behind Ten, got to the alleyway to see Ten down.

"Knocked him hard," Junil mentioned, "but he's still conscious. Let's keep him alive for now so we can interrogate."

Junil's right hand glowed blue, and he touched his right foot. Junil walked to Ten's side and kicked him in the stomach, making sure he'd drop unconscious. For insurance, he started to punch Ten's face until it was clear he was no longer awake.

"Please don't hurt me," Kaylin pleaded, "I'm not affiliated with Rose!"

"I don't like to hurt girls"—Kuril went back to Kaylin, who was still sitting at the end of the alleyway— "especially those who can't fight for themselves."

"You're letting me go?" Kaylin's face lightened up.

"No, but we won't hurt you," Kuril clarified, "please don't struggle."

"I understand, just please don't hurt me."

"I just said we weren't going to."

"Oh."

"I'll walk you back to our base of operations safely," Kuril stated, reaching out with his hand.

The girl took Kuril's hand, putting her trust in him. "Alright."

Junil picked up Ten's unconscious body and the four of them were headed toward the motel. Junil and Kuril exchanged looks a few times questioning why Kaylin was so accepting of the situation. Luckily, police influence in the outskirts of the city wasn't that big, so Junil didn't have to find himself in rundowns with an unconscious man on his back. As they approached the motel, Kaylin's hand lightened up in Kuril's hand. She was starting to feel a little more comfortable.

When the four approached the motel, they encountered a police officer.

"Mr. Junil, any explanation to why you're holding a body?" the officer asked.

"He's alive and well, but I'm never off of my job, you know?" Junil chuckled nervously.

"I'm going to need to see some identification for this man."

"Yeah, as if." Junil faked a laugh. "Who needs identification for a drunkard?"

"He's drunk?"

"And unconscious."

The officer took a good look at the body on Junil's back. "Poor guy's kids must be worried sick."

"That's why I'm here."

"You're right." Junil's charm seemed to work on the officer. "Go on."

Junil continued to carry Ten as Kuril held Kaylin's hand to guide her through the area. Compared to Kuril, Kaylin was only an inch and a half above his shoulders. Ten's body wasn't much for Junil's arms, though he was normal weight.

"We're here," Kuril told Kaylin, "you'll be okay."

She was silent as she entered the motel room, Kuril in front of her and Junil behind. Junil placed Ten on a chair and Kuril gently sat Kaylin on his bed.

"Do we have rope to restrain Ten?" Junil asked.

"No, I can run and get some though," Kuril offered.

"Please."

Kuril got up and walked to the exit of the motel room, "Should I bring Kaylin?"

"She doesn't seem like a fighter, so I'll take my chances with her around."

"Alright."

Kuril left the room, leaving Junil alone with an unconscious Ten and Kaylin, who was just sitting on Kuril's bed in an innocent manner.

"My name is Junil." The brown-haired man started to speak to Kaylin in a polite manner. "I'm a private detective."

"I've heard of you before." Kaylin recognized his name.

"I'm quite famous."

"No, Two talks about you a lot."

"Adam?"

"You two know each other?" Kaylin was surprised.

"We knew each other before Rose was established," Junil clarified, "we're still on good terms despite fighting a war against each other."

"You two were friends?"

"We grew up in the same orphanage." Junil sat on his bed across from Kaylin. "He was my friend."

"I wonder how you two went total opposite paths."

"The day we split was the defining moment." Junil clearly had an answer he didn't want to talk about. "Now we're both in two different departments."

"What's the intention with me?"

"What do you mean?"

"What do you want out of me being here? Rose won't just end with me as a hostage," Kaylin mentioned.

"Imagine capturing the center pawn on a chess board." Junil put it into an expression. "So you get the most important piece in the middle."

"I don't play chess, but sure."

"How old are you? You look very young adult-like, just a small physique."

"I'm 21."

"Same age as Kuril."

"Kuril?"

"The other man," Junil clarified, "the one who held your hand the way here."

"How old are you?"

"I'm 22."

"You're young for a famous detective." Kaylin took an interest in the detective. "How did you become so skilled?"

"When I was taken out of the orphanage, a prestigious family took me in and taught me the handles. The rest was pure skill."

The door opened and Junil peered over to see who it was. Kuril walked in with a rope and tossed it on Junil.

"Thanks, Kaylin wasn't trouble." Junil stood up and walked over to Ten. "You were rather quick."

"I know this motel owner. I just had to ask him for it."

Junil started to wrap the rope around Ten, and in a short amount of time, Ten was restrained to a chair. Junil looked over to see Kuril leaning against the wall.

"You clearly don't know where to sit." Junil gave a laugh, mocking his comrade. "That's hilarious."

"I'm nice to guests."

"Why do you like a girl affiliated with Rose?"

"I'm not affiliated with Rose by choice," Kaylin interrupted, "One and I are related by blood."

"One is the boss, correct?" Junil asked.

"Yes."

"What's your opinion on Rose?" Kuril joined in.

"I hate it," Kaylin admitted, "but no one should be dying over taking it down."

"Deal with reality." Kuril scoffed. "People will die."

"Then I embrace it."

Kuril and Junil were a little surprised by how easily she accepted reality. Kaylin's face was straight, it was almost confusing to the two of them.

"I want Rose gone more than you think," Kaylin continued, "you have no idea."

"Why?" Kuril pursued.

"The blood is on my hands." Kaylin's position hadn't changed. "The gang was made solely for me."

"Elaborate."

"I'm blind, weak, and I'm not fit to live in such a world. I am nothing except prey. James knew this, and made Rose for me. He wanted to give me the world, simply because the world wouldn't give me a fighting chance. I was destined to lose when I was born, and James has been doing everything he can to reverse that. The gang has a lot of money, they've made their lives comfortable, but I don't want this. I don't want to use bad means to achieve comfort, because I'd never truly be comfortable with that idea."

"Who's James?" Kuril asked.

"My brother."

"Why haven't you told James how you feel?"

"I have, but he seems to avoid my feelings. He thinks what he's doing is good for me and he has no care for the feelings of others."

"What do you think of James?"

"I love him. Throughout my entire life he's been continuously supporting me. He's saved my life countless times and he's given his all just for me. I have to appreciate his motives even if his means are awful."

"What if he died?"

"Rose will go down." Kaylin's tone of voice shifted to one that spoke with confidence, almost if she knew for certain. "But James won't."

"I see."

"So you're willing to work with us?" Junil asked.

"I am." Kaylin was joining forces with Kuril and Junil. "It's time for Rose to end."

"Are we going to need Ten?" Junil asked Kuril.

"We'll interrogate him, but it's likely we'll be killing him regardless."

"With Ten down, we have eleven more members to take down. Rose is truly in shambles right now, but their final five is a hard lineup to face."

"How do you know that?" Kuril asked.

"I've personally faced James before, and I know Two and Five."

"When did you face James?"

"I spotted him during a heist." Junil looked at Kaylin.

"You know Two and Five?" Kuril was surprised.

"We grew up in the same orphanage."

Kaylin pieced it together. "Five has never mentioned you, but I noticed she's somewhat close to Adam."

"Adam is Two?" Kuril asked.

"Yes," Junil answered, "and Five is named Anna."

"So you know their clouds and what they do I assume?"

"Yeah, I do."

"That's great to hear."

"Kuril." Junil held a poker face. "I will be the one to take Anna's life."

"Go ahead."

"That's all I want." Junil scanned Kaylin. "You're not a spy?"

"I'm not," Kaylin replied, "I want Rose down."

Kuril got up and grabbed a motel-provided notepad, "We'll need information on their members if we wish to win."

"I agree," Junil complied, "I'll be willing to discuss Adam and Anna."

"I can tell you as much as I know," Kaylin followed up, "but I won't discuss my cloud."

"You're not working with Rose, so what's the worry?" Kuril asked.

"There is no worry for both of you," Kaylin reassured them.

"Can you tell us about the clouds of Rose members?"

"Thirteen's cloud allows her hands to glow and cause a burning sensation through touch. She's swift and skilled at hand-to-hand combat, so she works at close-range."

"Next?"

"Twelve's cloud is—"

"Twelve is dead." Kuril cut Kaylin off.

"I see."

"Let's move on." Kuril calmed his voice, "Eleven?"

"Eleven's ability is scary." Kaylin's tone of voice became serious. "He can create portals to another world that bends to his will. One bad move and you can be sent to eternal hell."

"You're kidding." Junil felt a cold sweat take over. "Right?"

"I don't know how he has such immense power." Kaylin trembled at the mere thought of Eleven's power. "The fact of the matter is that he does."

Junil started to shiver and looked over at Kuril. "I can't fight that."

"What?" Kuril looked over to Junil in disbelief.

"I have a fear." Junil was barely able to get the words out. "I can't fight that. One mistake is…"

"Calm down, Junil." Kuril took control. "I'll take care of Eleven solo."

Junil had no response. He was controlling the shivering little by little, but it was true he was scared. It was exactly as Kaylin said: eternal hell. The idea of eternity spent suffering was enough to drive Junil to the edge, who feared infinity alone. Combine it with torment and he would practically break.

"Nine can manifest ice out of his hands." Kaylin continued the flow of the conversation. "On paths of ice he glides very well too."

"I see." Kuril was still taking notes. "Eight?"

"I'm pretty sure he has the ability to see through walls," Kaylin explained, "but as the rule for clouds go: he can't expend all his power, so he can only see through one or two walls at a time."

"Seven?"

"Can scan areas by leaving a trace of his cloud around it."

"How so?"

"Can track information and review what happened in a scene and who was involved."

"Is he the one who pinpointed Junil and I?"

"Yes."

"Interesting"—Kuril wrote more on the notepad— "what is Six's ability?"

"I don't know," Kaylin admitted, "he doesn't talk about it."

"And Junil, this is your spotlight now." Kuril looked over to him. "Five's ability?"

"Can create strings to shoot out of her hand. She handles it very well and uses it for battle tactics."

"Back to you, Kaylin."

"Four can shoot lasers out of his own index fingers," Kaylin told Kuril, "they're a lot more deadly than guns."

"How fast are the lasers?"

"Same speed as normal lasers."

"That's an issue. Can they break water?"

"It practically nullifies whatever's in the way."

"Shit." Kuril scratched his head. "Now for Three."

"Pyrokinetics, the ability to manipulate and manifest fire at will."

"And as for Two, Junil?"

"He can stop time for ten seconds at a time with the cooldown of three seconds in between." Junil looked at Kuril. "He's also a great fighter and tactician."

"As expected from one of Rose's top men."

"One can send anyone to an alternate reality by touching them for three seconds," Kaylin spoke. "His cloud is deadly. His speed is absurdly quick and he's a great fighter."

"I thought you couldn't see? How would you know about his speed?" Junil asked.

"I just hear it sometimes."

"Then he must be quick," Junil noted, "that's about everyone."

"None of these seem hard." Kuril paused for a second. "Except Eleven and the final few."

"I'm sorry," Junil spoke, "I can't face Eleven."

"Junil, just what does your cloud do?" Kuril struggled to piece it together.

Junil put his two hands up, showing Kuril his palms. The

right palm had a blue plus symbol and the left had an orange minus symbol.

"My cloud revolves around the hands," Junil said. "If I grab something with my left hand, I can nullify or weaken power in that object, as I did with Ten's head earlier, shutting down the major sections of his brain."

"And I suppose the right does the opposite?"

"My right hand powers objects, so if I touch my left hand with my right and power it up, my punch from my left hand will be stronger."

"How long does it last?"

"Ten seconds, three second cooldown. If I use the left hand, the cooldown still applies to the right hand, and I can't use them at the same time."

"Ten seconds, three seconds." Kuril recognized those two numbers. "Just like Adam."

"There's no correlation between us when it comes to cloud abilities. Those numbers hold no significance to me."

"I see."

"Kaylin." Junil changed the topic to her. "Why can't we know your cloud?"

"Because you won't sleep peacefully tonight if you do."

"What does that mean?" Junil folded his arms.

"That's part of my ability."

"I understand," Junil said, "so you're lying."

"I'm not."

"Then prove it. What is your cloud?" Junil could tell Kaylin was bluffing. She didn't have a cloud.

Kaylin was caught in her own lie. "So," Kaylin said, "when is Ten going to die?"

"You sound like Kuril," Junil said, chuckling, "why such a rush?"

"I think Rose deserves death, both the members and the organization."

"Even your brother?" Junil asked.

"My feelings for my brother are different," Kaylin admitted, "I don't want him dead."

"That's only reasonable, considering you're related."

"I see her point," Kuril butted in, "why isn't Ten dead yet?"

Junil took out his pistol and tossed it to Kuril. "Do the honors!"

"We can't have suspicion dragged on us." Kuril wasn't as easygoing as Junil. "We have to kill him somewhere else."

"Just drown him in the toilet." Junil wasn't in the mood. "The cops will trust that he's a Rose member I dealt with. Information won't reach Rose."

"If it does?"

"It won't."

"So be it."

Kuril brought the tied up chair with Ten's unconscious body on it to the bathroom, where he placed it in order for Ten's head to be completely submerged in the toilet.

"He'll die soon," Kuril pointed out, sighing and coming out of the bathroom, "so we'll have four out of fifteen dead."

In the corner of the room, Ten stood with his arms folded and right leg on the wall. "Four out of fifteen?"

Kuril's eyes widened as he looked toward where the voice spoke, but saw no one. He looked back at Junil, hoping the detective would confirm his belief that Ten was right there. As Junil awkwardly looked at the Violet, both of them realized they were not on similar ground.

"Did you not hear Ten?" Kuril asked.

"Of course not."

"He just spoke in the corner of the room!" Kuril pointed toward one of the walls. "Right there!"

"You're hallucinating."

"I'm not. I heard him."

Junil stood up and immediately directed himself into the bathroom, where he saw Ten's head submerged into the toilet.

Following behind him was Kuril, who glanced over Junil's shoulder in disbelief. Ten was still there.

"That can't be," Kuril said, leaving the bathroom and looking into the same corner where Ten was.

A hand touched Kuril's shoulder as the haunting voice revealed itself once again. "What a shame."

Kuril turned around as quickly as he could to apprehend Ten, but he wasn't there. Was he really ever there? Why was Kuril the only person who could feel Ten's presence? Was he hallucinating?

"You had to see or hear him that time, Junil."

The detective scratched the back of his head. "You need some sleep."

Kuril began to doubt himself as he kept looking at the corner where he first heard Ten. "Yeah, I guess."

"Hasn't even been a week yet." Junil groaned. "So exhausted."

"I feel like napping." Kuril was tired too.

"Let's get some rest, no one will find us right now."

"Let's hope they never do."

"What about me?" Kaylin asked.

"Do you want to nap?" Junil followed up with a question.

"Nothing better to do," Kaylin said, sighing.

"Take Kuril's bed, he'll take the motel floor."

"That's not very nice," Kaylin pointed out, "is it okay with you, Kuril?"

"It's fine with me, just a blanket and a pillow is all I need." Kuril seemed okay with it.

Junil tossed his pillow over to Kuril.

"Can I get a blanket?" Kuril asked.

Junil groaned. "Really?"

"You have two of them."

Junil threw one of his blankets across the room. "It's a shame that I have to sleep with one blanket."

Without another word between the two, they decided to finally nap. They were exhausted, both physically and mentally. Such a load could only be taken off with alcohol or sleep, but they chose the latter. Kaylin caught the memo from the silence and fell asleep as well. No one was keeping lookout, but no one wanted to.

"Hey, Adam."

"What is it, James?"

"Twelve is dead, Ten and Kaylin are missing."

"So is the Blooming Day finally reaching near?"

"I suppose so."

In a rusty, rundown building by the outskirts of Velindas, Adam and James were hiding out. The other Rose members usually did whatever they wanted during the day and night, whether it was to binge drink, shop, or blend in with everyday activities. The gang almost never had one spot they were at all the time, but Adam and James usually stood together.

"The Blooming Day," Adam mentioned, "will it really work?"

"I know it will, or else everything would be for nothing."

"Who has Kaylin in captivity?"

"Likely those two people Seven told us about, Junil and Kuril."

"I know Junil wouldn't hurt a woman." Adam oozed with confidence. "So she's safe."

"Do you think Junil killed Ten?"

"Probably," Adam said.

"As long as Kaylin is safe, then the Blooming Day plan will go through."

"I hope this is worth it."

Back at the abandoned church, the doors finally opened for the first time since Twelve hit the ground.

"Well, well, well. If it isn't Twelve!" Three laughed. "Oh, where are you?"

Three looked around, unable to spot Twelve. He started to make chirping noises to taunt the white-haired girl.

Three cupped his hands around his mouth. "Here, kitty, kitty, kitty!"

"Shut up," she responded, laying down on a church pew out of Three's line of sight.

"Faking your death really isn't easy, huh?"

She scoffed and sat up, looking at him.

"How did you do it?" the man in the blazer asked, swooping his straight, black hair back.

"I used a bubble to instantly nullify the bullet's existence the second it was fired at me. I wasn't informed it was going to be shot, but I knew detective Junil was behind the church waiting to shoot me."

"My, oh, my, how did you know?"

"I placed a tiny bubble on him. As you already know, I can track where my bubbles are at all times."

"How did you react?"

"The bubble was so tiny, I made it creep into the gun, where I reformed it around the bullet. I was essentially tracking the bullet the entire time."

Three spread his arms out. "You lived! You deserve a hug!"

"Shut up."

Clearing his voice, Three finally decided to get serious. "Now that you're no longer affiliated with Rose, what is your real name?"

"Kyra Redd."

"William Lewis."

"Great," Kyra replied, "I assume this means that you won't be affiliating with Rose anymore?"

"I'll continue associating myself with Rose to help proceed with the investigation we're conducting."

"Interesting," she replied.

William looked up at the ceiling of the church. "Thirteen is going to try to kill me, huh?"

"You'll manage."

"I promise I won't hurt her."

"I already knew you wouldn't."

William looked back over at Kyra. "What do you mean?"

"You're more respectable than you look, even though I constantly give you shit for it."

"You're more of a dick than you look, even though you play the innocent role."

"Thanks," Kyra replied.

"Thirteen is definitely going to fight that blond boy, it's only a matter of time."

Back at Velindas' other side of the outskirts, the motel was greeted with the awakening of Junil, who napped for about two hours. Kaylin was awake at the time, doing absolutely nothing.

"Kaylin, you're a guest," Junil whispered as to not wake Kuril up, "if you need something just ask. I can tell you're bored."

"I'm just thinking," Kaylin responded.

"I get it." Junil raised himself out of bed. "I'm going to the vending machine for a drink real quick."

"See you in a few minutes."

Junil left the motel room, accidentally closing the door loudly. Kuril rose up, believing a threat was at hand.

"Who's there?" Kuril asked.

"Junil left," Kaylin answered, "he's getting a drink."

Kuril, without responding, stood up. He stretched his body out, feeling sore from all that combat without a massage. His physical state was wearing thin.

"Hey." Kuril took out his phone. "We slept for two hours. It's nearing nighttime now."

"What time is it?" Kaylin asked.

"Half past eight." Kuril gave out a yawn. "I need a drink too. Want something?"

"Surprise me."

"Sounding like me now." Kuril let out a smile. "I'll get you some bottled tea then."

Kuril left the room, headed toward the vending machine by the parking lot. He saw Junil taking a sip of a bottled soft drink by the soda dispenser and walked past him without a word. The two were so similar, words didn't need to be spoken between them. Kuril slipped two dollars into the vending machine, picking two bottles of tea.

"Junil." Kuril broke the silence. "How do you feel about Kaylin?"

"It's hard to trust her, but I do."

"It's just that… who else can we trust?"

"No one," Junil responded, "but we have us."

"If she's right about the next cloud we face, I'll put my trust in her hands."

"That sounds good with me"—Junil took another sip—"otherwise we'll have to eliminate her."

"That would be a shame, she's a nice girl."

"I don't hurt girls. If I must, I will kill them, but I won't hurt them."

"So it'd be my job if you can't make it swift?"

"Yeah." Junil was glad Kuril got the memo. "I doubt the worst is approaching, though."

"Having optimism will assure victory," Kuril responded.

"Not always, but I enjoy the attitude."

"Shall we head back?"

"One more thing I want to ask." Junil took a deep look into Kuril's eyes. "What was life back at your home like?"

Kuril was silent for a few seconds, followed by a swallow. "It was peaceful. I was next in line to become the head of the village. My teacher, who was the head of the village, taught me how to use my cloud and how to defend others. I was pretty strong before the slaughter, and afterwards, I exponentially grew in strength."

"Do you think it's enough to take down Rose?"

"I don't know how strong the final five are, so I can't judge."

"I see." Junil sighed. "Go on with the story."

"In my free time, I did whatever I pleased, whether it was hanging out with friends or climbing the trees nearby. I even bullied a girl to the point where she abandoned the village. She was the daughter of my teacher."

"That's mad fucked up," Junil said, "what happened to her?"

"I have no idea. Whether it was physical or mental, I made sure to assert dominance over her. It was really messed up, but I moved past that."

"Regret only holds people back." Junil let a smile out. "If only you could see her again and ask for forgiveness."

"If I see her again, I'll ask. If she's still alive, she's the only other Violet living."

"What about me?"

"You're only half Violet. You don't count, plus you were raised in the city."

"Why wasn't she the next head of the village? She's the daughter of the head."

"It's only for guys."

"I see."

"Anything else?"

"Your teacher," Junil went on, "what did he look like?"

"Tall, blond hair like mine, but he put it in a ponytail. He also had this necklace." Kuril took the necklace out of his pocket and showed it to Junil. "Why do you ask?"

"That may have been my father," Junil revealed, "who left my mother when she needed him most. I hope he's rotting in Hell."

"I'm sorry to hear that, I know he wasn't the best man."

"That means the girl you used to bully is my half-sister."

"What does that mean to you?" Kuril asked.

"She's alive." Junil let out a chuckle. "She took part in the massacre of your people."

"You're kidding, right?" Kuril's eyes were filled with shock, guilt returning to his body. His legs were still, but you could tell he was trembling inside.

"I'm always in direct contact with Adam," Junil explained, "and he told me about her. Apparently, only James knew this information, but James told Adam, and now I know. This information is best fit for you."

"Mia... is alive?" Kuril barely let the words escape his mouth.

"She's alive, and she's Thirteen."

Kuril regained control over his own body, "That means I have to eliminate her."

"You can do that," Junil complied, "but I can't fight tomorrow."

As the blond Kuril blinked, he saw a figure stand right in front of him. It was none other than Ten, who kept popping up out of seemingly nowhere. Kuril froze and turned his head to Junil slowly.

"What's wrong?" Junil asked, turning his head to Kuril.

"You can't see him, right?"

"Is this about Ten?"

Kuril nodded.

Junil looked back into the view. "If the hallucinations aren't hurting you, then just let it be. It's probably an after effect of his cloud. I doubt you'll be damaged at all. We have information to sort out."

"Yeah, you're right."

"As I was saying, you can kill Thirteen. I won't be fighting anyone tomorrow."

Kuril shifted his head slightly. "Why not?"

"I have to meet up with Adam." Junil let out a sigh. "He says it's important."

"Who cares? He's just a dirty Rose member!"

"He's more than a Rose member." Junil clenched his drink harder. "He's a man of justice. He's done a lot for this city, but you don't know him like I do."

"Whatever."

A few seconds passed by. The pressure in the air rose as the two men differed in opinions, almost as if that one judgement were two clashing seas, wave crashing into wave. However, despite no words being spoken, the tides calmed down as the duo relaxed.

"Time to go back?"

"Yeah."

Junil and Kuril walked back to the motel room. When they entered, Kaylin was in the same spot, eyes still closed. Kaylin didn't like to open her eyes, because she knew how useless it would be. Many blind people are the same way regarding keeping their eyelids down.

"Here's your tea." Kuril placed a bottle of tea into Kaylin's hands.

"Thank you." Kaylin smiled.

Junil and Kuril exchanged glances, but quickly dismissed whatever was going through their brains. In truth, they thought such a smile was suspicious, but keeping suspicion was a bad idea for them.

"Eleven." Kuril brought up an actual topic. "Where can we find him?"

"He's usually with his girl in an apartment, but I'm not sure where."

"I see."

"Kaylin, if you know anything about his identity, I might be able to find his apartment." Junil joined in.

"I don't know anything more than his cloud and the type of person he is."

"Where can we find Nine?" Kuril asked, jumping to the next opponent.

"He's usually drinking by a bar called Zipline," Kaylin answered.

"Then that's our spot, Junil."

"Can't show up, meeting with Adam."

"Oh, I forgot." Kuril looked toward the bathroom. "What's going to happen with the body?"

Junil looked at the ceiling. "I can dispose of it at night."

"Is that fine with you?" Kuril asked.

"Yeah."

"Great." Kuril hopped back on his floor. "It's time to sleep."

"You just woke up from a nap." Junil sighed.

"I tend to sleep easily."

"Good for you, some of us can't."
"Not my fault." Kuril turned over. "Good night."
Ten stood over Kuril. "Good night, Kuril."
Kuril closed his eyes knowing it wasn't real.

CHAPTER IV

The next day had already come, and as Junil and Adam planned, they were going to meet up. This time, they met up at the Zipline bar, where Nine frequents. Junil sat alone at the bar, where Adam had not yet arrived.

The Zipline bar was not exactly famous, yet it was known on the business side of Velindas due to the solid crowd it gets each day. When you're working in the modern day, you sometimes need to cool off with some alcohol. Also, it's apparently really easy to pass with a fake ID, but that is definitely not the reason people frequent Velindas' classy bar. The polished indoors were combined with dim, yet yellow tinted lighting throughout the entire day. According to some people, the light turns a shade red during the night, a possible tribute to the colors of the sky during the sunrise and sunset.

"Get me a classic Martini." Junil sighed. "My man hasn't showed up yet."

"The alcoholic?" the bartender laughed.

"No, not that one."

The bartender grabbed his two stainless steel cups and mixed away. Junil watched in astonishment as the man behind the counter shook the two cups together to mix the drink. Junil was never really one for alcohol, so the entire process was not only interesting to observe, but fascinating to watch. The bartender placed the detective's drink next to him with a smile, one that radiated passion for his job and delight for serving another happy customer.

Junil took his drink, smiled, and took a sip. "It's wonderful. I don't even know how alcoholic beverages work. I just ordered the only one I know."

"Not even a beer?" the bartender asked.

"I forgot that existed."

The two shared a laugh, Junil took another sip, and the door opened.

"I apologize for being late, my dear."

"Adam, it's so nice to see you." Junil's face glowed.

"You aren't the type to get flustered, not sure why I tried." Adam chuckled, taking a seat next to Junil.

"'My dear' isn't much of a nickname," Junil admitted, "so why am I here?"

"Well, I've been meaning to tell—"

"Are we safe here? Is Nine coming?"

"I told Nine that I had business around noon, so I told him he can come later tonight." Adam looked up at the bartender. "I'll take what he's having."

"Alright then"—Junil took another sip— "what is it?"

"Kaylin." Adam's face grew serious.

"One's sister? What about her?"

"She's gone missing." Adam's face took a brooding turn.

"Why is this my matter?"

"Junil, you're the world's greatest detective." Adam stared into Junil's eyes. "Please find her."

"And if I told you I knew where she was?"

"I'd ask you where, nothing more. I'd never hurt my husband."

"We aren't married, Adam." Junil laughed. "Good try."

"Are you still in love with Anna? Even after what she did to Mr. Brown?" Adam's expression quickly turned dramatic, enough for Junil to easily read that he was kidding.

"Let's not discuss Anna." Junil's grip on his drink tightened.

"I understand." Adam's drink was served to him at the exact moment. "Thank you."

"About Kaylin." Junil stared into his Martini, "I know where she is."

"Where?"

"I have her in my custody." Junil took another sip, noticing how shallow a Martini glass was, and how little he had left of his drink. "She's safe."

"That's good, I'll tell One as soon as I can."

"Adam, I want to eliminate all of Rose."

"Does that include me? I feel betrayed."

"I don't want to do it, but chances are, we'll cross paths eventually."

"So is this a truce?" Adam laughed, raising his glass.

"A truce between you and I, brothers forever." Junil smiled, and two glasses clicked together to symbolize brotherhood, though they were not actual brothers by blood.

"Two friends on two different sides of war." Adam chuckled, "Isn't it ironic?"

"I have a request for you." Junil's fingers were gliding across the glass. "Can you somewhat arrange ways for Kuril and I to get in battle with Rose members?"

"Kuril is your friend, correct?"

"Acquaintance."

"Sheesh, stubborn."

"Ten is dead, and I know you don't care."

"That's right." Adam took a sip out of his drink. "A Martini is pretty basic, Junil."

Junil clenched his drink. "Help Kuril and I arrange ways to get rid of Rose members."

"What's in it for me?"

"I know you don't care about Rose." Junil faced Adam. "They're pawns to you."

"And?"

"You're plotting something." Junil's eyes were scanning Adam's face. "What is it?"

"None of your business."

"Then I'll resort to violence to make sure I can eliminate Rose."

Adam gave a blank look. "What do you mean?"

"If I die right here," Junil spoke, "I've already let Kuril know that Kaylin is a threat."

"So you're blackmailing me?"

"That's exactly right. She's the pawn in the middle of the board."

"I'll comply then." Adam's aura became very dark, almost shifting the mood of the entire bar. "If she gets hurt..."

"She'll be fine as long as I can see my goal through."

"Fight in areas with less people, but areas that aren't suspicious."

"You'll arrange for them to show up?"

Adam shrugged. "I'll tell who is showing up, you choose the spot and the time."

"You're a good man, Adam, it's no wonder I fell in love with you," Junil joked.

"Don't toy with my heart." Adam let out a chuckle. "I might take you seriously one day."

"Adam," Junil spoke, "if I swung that way, I'd surely be in love with you."

"I'll take that." Adam took a sip and choked on his drink. "You don't swing that way?"

Junil cleared his throat. "Too busy for romance or sex. Never really saw the appeal."

"Are you kidding? Romance is amazing!"

Junil sighed. "Indoor voice, Adam."

"Woe is me."

"You and One are going to be different cases. I know we can't just assault One. I have no intention of hurting you. I don't know what will happen, but something will happen."

"We get there when we get there."

Junil looked around at the empty bar, bartender on his phone, paying no mind to Junil and Adam. He probably had no idea who Junil was, since not everyone was involved in Velindas politics. The city had corrupt officials and politicians, so no one really cared about the political situation.

"Anna." Junil continued the conversation. "I'm going to kill her."

"I thought you didn't like harming girls?"

"Never anything against killing them, especially for a Rose member."

"That's very fair." Adam took another sip of his drink.

"Make sure Nine shows up here tonight, Kuril wants to take care of Thirteen."

"So you'll take out Nine tonight, and Kuril will go for Thirteen's head?"

"Tell Thirteen to meet him in the dunes outside the city, where they can fight in peace. Both of them will comply."

"How come? No suspicion on my end?"

"Tell Thirteen that Kuril was the one who requested the battle. She'll take that no matter what. There's beef to be settled between the two."

"Oh, so history between them? Similar to you and Anna?"

"It's way different for them."

"I see." Adam spun the ice in his glass. "Thirteen isn't coping with Twelve's death too well. I believe they were in love."

"Thirteen knows?"

"Yeah, but she's been a little strange recently."

Junil started to tap his fingers on the bar table. "Shit."

Adam's phone buzzed as he took it out of his pocket. "I can't tell what Thirteen is going through."

"A new message?"

"One asked me to play cards with him to pass the time before our next mission."

"So we'll be headed out?"

"Let me ask if he wants another man in the party."

"Pause." Junil spoke. "You're inviting me to play cards with a man who probably wants me dead."

"He wants you alive."

"That doesn't make sense."

"It does." Adam typed out a text on his phone and hit the send button, then turned to Junil. "Play cards with us."

"I think I'll pass."

"Boring and cautious, not the life I'd choose."

"I'm trying to not die," Junil remarked, "but does he really want me alive?"

"I don't know, but my best bet is that he wants you dead."

"Oh, that's great to know that you could've killed me," Junil let out a sigh.

"I wouldn't let him kill you so quickly."

"Whatever, let's head out."

Junil got up from the bar and Adam left behind a sum of cash for the bartender. They exited the room and headed out onto the Velindas streets.

"We part ways here. Give me a call when things are in motion. Remember, Nine meets me here at midnight. Thirteen should meet Kuril at the entrance of the Velindas Hotel, where they'll head to that dune together to fight."

"Both are at midnight?"

"Exactly." Junil started walking. "If I don't get a call, Kaylin dies."

"Alright." Adam walked in the opposite direction.

Both of the childhood friends created a deal, and there were going to be fight arrangements coming around. For Junil, getting rid of Rose was the top priority. As for Adam, Kaylin's safety was at the top of his list. The only thing Rose members could do in this situation is react accordingly to what was ahead of them.

Arriving back at the motel, Junil jumped on his bed. Kuril and Kaylin were still in there, doing absolutely nothing. The television was on, broadcasting the news. Kuril was watching it, but Kaylin could only listen.

"Is that you, Junil?"

"Yes, Kaylin, it's me."

"What did you talk about with Adam?" Kaylin asked.

"We discussed the ethics of capitalism and how it fails society."

"Not funny. What did you actually talk about?"

"None of your business."

Kaylin groaned. "Be that way."

"Hey, Kuril." Junil looked over at Kuril sitting in a chair.

"What is it?" Kuril responded.

"You got a date tonight," Junil blurted out.

"What?"

"At midnight, you'll be meeting Thirteen at the Velindas Hotel."

"What the hell?" Kuril rose from his chair.

"The goal is obvious: eliminate her." Junil was giving commands like this was his base of operations.

"Of course that's the goal, but you couldn't warn me earlier?" Kuril was a little agitated.

"Adam and I arranged a deal today. I won't go into the specifics, but he's going to help me arrange fights and ambushes on the Rose members."

"That's great to hear, but I need to prepare for tonight."

"I got a date too, but it's the alcoholic Nine."

"Do I have a date?" Kaylin asked.

"A date with the eye doctor?" Junil bursted out laughing.

"Junil, you can't just say that!" Kuril's eyebrows tensed up.

"Lighten up, Kuril, he was just joking around." Kaylin giggled.

Junil calmed down after his laughing outburst. "See? She gets it."

"Whatever." Kuril scoffed.

"Go and prepare," Junil told Kuril, "I won't need to, so catch me sleeping here."

"You won't need to warm up?" Kuril questioned Junil's confidence.

"My ability should work well against ice, it's kinetic energy."

"So you'll basically melt ice with your right hand?" Kuril was interested.

"It's a matchup I can't lose."

"You're smart for choosing Nine," Kuril admitted, "I'll go and get ready, work up my reflexes at a batting cage or something."

"Have fun." Junil waved as Kuril headed for the exit.

"Thank you, Junil. Now I can end Thirteen's life."

The door closed behind Kuril, and the room was filled with silence.

"What a questionable line," Junil said.

"He's quite the broody and serious guy," Kaylin noted.

"Kuril has been through a lot. He has so many mental scars that he has almost no emotion. That's as much as I can read from him."

"The only way he'll ever be whole again is if Rose goes down, but I doubt he'll ever be normal again."

"I don't think he cares about being normal."

"What do you mean?" Kaylin asked.

"He has no care for the future, he just wants Rose gone."

"One step at a time for him?"

"No, it's more like the future is meaningless. It's almost as if he's jumping into a fire."

"Don't say that, I don't want to see him hurt."

"Aww, someone's in love!"

"Or it's called being a good person?" Kaylin responded.

"I'm joking around."

Kaylin gulped. "I don't want him to die."

"He's too smart to be killed."

"I hope so."

"So smart he'll probably kill himself."

Kaylin felt an overbearing chill across her body. "What do you mean?"

"He's destructive."

"He doesn't care about himself either, huh?"

"Yeah."

As the time flew out of the window, Kuril was approaching one of the biggest moments of his life. Junil was still in bed. It was thirty minutes before midnight, both men anticipating a fight. Kuril had a personal grudge to solve. Junil just wanted to wind down the number of Rose members.

"Aren't you going to fight Nine?" Kaylin asked.

"Oh, so now you know what time it is?"

"I don't, I just know it's getting late."

"Fine, I'll be on my way. Stay safe tonight, and remember that Kuril and I will return."

"Be careful."

"Sure thing, see you later." Junil shut the door behind him.

The final bell was ringing for two souls. The reaper was ready to take two lives at the gate of night, but there were four people fighting. Blood was going to be shed, and Junil and Kuril had no intention of having their blood spill into the hands of their enemies.

Kuril was waiting at the entrance of the Velindas Hotel. He saw a brown-haired girl approaching him, eyes filled with the intent to kill.

"Are you Mia?"

"Kuril, you've grown."

"Before we head out to an open place to fight, I want to apologize."

"I don't care about your apology." Mia let out a sigh. "Let's just go."

Kuril started walking alongside Mia. "I was an awful child. You were so mature, yet you couldn't be the next head of the village just because you were a girl. My bullying was dismissed as a guy showing he had a crush on a girl, but in truth, I wanted to make you feel awful. I don't know why."

"I don't forgive you, and I'm going to end your life as the finale for the Violet."

"I understand, but I have no intention of letting you win. I will kill you."

"We aren't really big with words, huh?"

"We're more similar than you—"

"Never compare me to scum like you."

"I apologize." Kuril looked toward the path ahead.

The road ahead was going to be one of silence for the two. Walking forward, they left behind everything: history, grudges, desires. There was nothing left for the two besides to fight to the death. Their eyes were empty, their souls were forever tarnished, and their hearts were weak. They had one focus and one focus only: to take the life of the person next to them.

On the other side of Velindas, more by the business end of the city, the Zipline bar had very few people in it. One of those people was Nine, who was told that the famous detective Junil was going to be there at midnight. The door opened, and in came Junil.

"Excuse me, bartender, I'll have to escort someone out of here tonight." Junil scanned the room.

"And you are?" the bartender asked.

"I was here earlier today," Junil confirmed, "I'm Junil, the detective who makes the news a lot."

"Isn't that interesting?" Nine stood up from his seat.

"Someone's pride got in the way of an immediate ambush. I didn't know you at all, Nine."

"How did you know I was going to be here tonight?" Nine asked.

"Doesn't matter, you die tonight. They don't call me the Phantom of Velindas for nothing."

"Take this outside," the bartender grumpily demanded.

"I apologize," Junil said, directing Nine to head outside.

The two of them headed outside, ready to fight.

"We should go into an alleyway," Nine recommended, "I wouldn't want the public to see Junil dead on the street."

"Yeah, I don't want them to see my corpse either. I apologize, let's be on our way then."

"Stop playing mind games. You suck at them."

"Sorry, I meant to say that I'm winning this fight."

"Sure you are, pal." Nine considered Junil's words to be a joke.

In the alleyway next to the Zipline bar, there was an empty lot. It was useful for fistfights that happened after drunkards got at each other's throats. Though no one knows who exactly owns this empty lot, it's unused and ends up being the home of a lot of fights. Junil and Nine walked into that empty lot through the alleyway, preparing to kill.

"It's not very spacious, but it works," Junil said.

Nines faced his palms out. "Time to die, Junil."

"That's the Phantom of Velindas to you."

Nines summoned two icicles from the palms of his hand, grabbing them as sharpened spears. Junil stood still across the empty lot, already knowing his victory was ensured.

"Before we start," Junil interrupted, "I have a switchblade in my pocket. That's my sole weapon."

"You're cocky, Junil, that'll be your downfall."

"Hallowed be my name, the legendary Junil doesn't fail."

"Oh, now you're a saint?"

"I'm this city's last hope against Rose," Junil said, "so perhaps."

"Let's start this fight." Nine gave Junil a sardonic smile. "You piss me off."

Nine charged at Junil. Taking out his switchblade and placing it in his right hand, Junil waited for Nine to get closer. Nine's icicles were at both sides of Junil. To the average person, this would be Junil's demise, but to Junil, it was an easy way to start a retaliation. Running toward the wall behind him, Junil jumped off the wall to distract Nine, making Nine think that Junil had a plan. Junil's real plan was simple and working: fool Nine into thinking Junil had an actual plan.

Nine stood in place and waited to defend from Junil's attack, expecting it from the legs. Junil put his left leg ahead of his other limbs to symbolize that he was going for a kick, but quickly put his upper body forward once Nine prepared to defend a kick. Finishing a flip and landing behind Nine, Junil immediately ducked and grabbed Nine's left shoulder with left hand, disabling it for ten seconds.

"In ten seconds, you will be able to move your arm again," Junil said, noticing Nine was planning to jab him with the right icicle.

Junil fell back, took out the switchblade handle, and charged back at Nine. With only one arm open, Nine had no option but to retreat until his arm was stable again. Dropping the right icicle, Nine shot a dart of ice straight for Junil's head. In an unexpected turn of events for Junil, he found the opportunity to take out the left hand.

Junil couldn't dodge the dart of ice in time while also taking out the left hand, so he played his cards in a way that would damage himself and his opponent. Taking the dart of ice head on into his right shoulder, Junil's right arm was pierced.

Running straight at Nine, who now had nothing in both hands, Junil grabbed his immobile left arm with his right hand and activated the switchblade in his left hand, jabbing it straight into Nine's left hand. The pain of applying pressure to his pierced right arm caused Junil to yelp, but he didn't wimp out. Junil took out the switchblade and retreated back to the other end of the lot. Junil, who was dominant with his right hand, had learned to use his left hand when he couldn't use his right hand in combat.

Though he wasn't ambidextrous, he was proficient enough with his left hand to get a stab in.

"Can you make ice now? I'm a little thirsty. I could use a Martini on the rocks, you know?" Junil joked.

Nine looked at his hand.

The detective's smug aura radiated through the empty lot. "Oh, I forgot, your arm is numb and you're unable to process pain in that area. Time's up just about now."

Nine started screaming in agony, now feeling the pain in his hand. A stream of negative emotions flowed through Nine's mind, all fueled by his hatred for the man in the trench coat who was grinning at the pain he inflicted on him. A deadly stare was directed toward Junil, one that gave the detective a boost in ego. Nine was now leaking with negativity, stemming from his intent to humiliate and kill Junil. Ice came out of his only free hand, forming a spear-like rod, ready to take the detective out in one hit.

"I have nothing to do tonight. Best time for you to kill me." Junil's cockiness was clearly overwhelming Nine.

Nine went toward Junil, charging with caution. Nine was only holding the spear with one hand, but it was light. It was an easy weapon to impale Junil with. Junil dropped off to the side and dodged the jab. Nine was in so much pain that he could barely focus on anything except his hand, which was bleeding out. Jab after jab, Junil repeatedly dodged, noticing Nine getting slower.

Nine had a second part to his ability that Junil didn't know: he could melt the ice he created. Nine was reaching the end of the line, practically just hoping someone would show up to save him. Nine melted the ice dart in Junil's arm, causing the blood to start flowing. Junil held his right arm, which was starting to shake. His trench coat was growing a darker shade of brown.

As blood rushed out, Junil grew distracted. His eyes adjusted toward Nine again, angered at what was done to his arm. His eyes were sharp, almost like a cat. Nine was his prey, who had just disgraced and humiliated him.

Nine took the chance to take a jab at Junil, who was still grasping onto his arm. Junil rolled across the lot to avoid the jab, but was met with the spear up to his face when he tripped trying to regain his balance.

"Now you know how it feels." Nine caught his breath.

"What do you mean?"

"Your arm and my hand are similar now, and I'll kill you for what you just did."

"You're confusing me." Junil loosened his grip on his arm.

Nine grew furious. "What don't you fucking understand?"

"We aren't similar." Junil was being genuine. "I'm way above you. I'm a savior for this city, and I'm all they have."

"Are you fucking stupid?" Nine was taunting Junil, but Junil didn't seem to care.

"And furthermore, you can't even kill me." Junil wasn't joking, he thought he couldn't die by the hands of Nine. "I've won anyways."

"Bullshit."

"Behind you."

Nine took a peek behind him, in which Junil, on the ground, went for a sweep kick. Using his left arm as support, Junil stood back up again, and suddenly, the tables were turned. Junil felt a pain in his right arm and clutched it with his left hand, where Nine took advantage and got back up using his right arm.

Junil charged right at Nine before ice could be summoned. Nine created an ice dagger with the right hand in a hurry, but at that point, it was too late for both of them. Junil's hip was stabbed, but Nine's right arm went numb. The two men landed their respective hits.

"You fought well"—Junil grabbed Nine by the hair with his left hand and threw him into the ground—"but you've lost."

Nine's right arm was numb, and now there were no hands for Nine to summon ice from. Nine realized what this meant for him: he was unable to use his cloud for the next ten seconds.

"Doctor, scalpel." Junil let out a fake laugh, taking the switchblade back out, blood stained on the steel, "I don't think the patient will make it!"

"Please, don't do it." Nine couldn't get up. It would take too long to use his left elbow to support himself to stand, and he was unable to use his left hand, as it was impaled.

"I think we need to dig into his hand, doctor."

"Please!"

Junil stabbed the right palm of Nine. Both hands had holes in them, making Junil question how ice would be summoned.

"You'll feel it in a few seconds."

"No! I don't want to feel it! Not again! Please just—"

The empty lot was filled with screams yet again due to Nine beginning to feel the pain of an impaled palm again. He was on the ground, practically rolling, unable to control himself. Filled with fear for his own life, he knew his battle was over.

"Help! Anyone, please!" Nine screamed as loud as he could.

"I didn't think I'd have to kill you so fast." Junil sighed. "Say goodbye before help arrives."

Nine tried to use a last attempt to save himself by summoning ice, but it only filled the wounds of his hands, eventually jamming the area up, causing Nine to be rendered useless in a fight. He screamed in even more pain, the ice clogging the inside of his wound.

"The Phantom of Velindas has to put you in your place." Junil smiled, making sure the last thing Nine saw was his face. "I'll see you in Hell. And by the way, whether I fooled you or not, I could have just melted your ice spear anyways. You didn't have a chance to start. I just wanted to have fun."

The switchblade was placed in one final spot, Nine's throat. It was over. Nine's body fell limp. Footsteps rushed into the empty lot with flashlights on. They immediately noticed Junil hovering over Nine's body. Men in police uniforms took notice of Junil.

"It was a member of Rose." Junil grabbed the wound in his hip. "It's a gruesome sight this time around."

"Junil, you've been doing a lot against Rose lately," one of the cops spoke, "just how much can you do?"

"The Phantom of Velindas rests during the day, not the night. No one should touch my territory at night. Rose just stepped into the lion's den."

"Someone call an ambulance, Junil needs medical assistance," the police officer directed the other two officials beside him.

One of them took out their handheld receiver and immediately contacted for medical support, officially stating it was Junil who needed it. Junil was losing a lot of blood after the dagger had melted from the death of Nine. Unable to keep his eyes open after the fight, Junil fell over onto the ground next to Nine.

Kuril and Thirteen had finally reached a good spot to fight at.

"It's empty over here," Kuril told Thirteen, "are you ready?"

"Today is the day that I get my revenge." Thirteen walked a few meters away. "Are you ready?"

"Yeah."

Thirteen swiftly took action and jolted toward Kuril. Leaping on top of him, she pinned him down with her legs and tried putting her hands on his face. Thirteen's cloud, the ability to burn anything with her palms, was deadly when combined with her fighting style. Kuril, in his attempt to resist, grabbed her by the wrists, where she couldn't use her ability.

In a standoff between the two, Kuril noticed his strength growing weaker, trying to hold up a force going downwards. While Thirteen applied pressure, Kuril took one final push forward, where he broke free. Kuril extended his right arm to the side of him and let water drip out. His tactic was simple: if Thirteen got a grip on him, he'd use his ability to become water and regain his composure at that checkpoint, acting as teleportation.

Kuril moved away from that checkpoint so he could gain distance if he needed to use it. Thirteen took another charge at

Kuril, pinning him down again. Kuril became water and regained himself at the checkpoint he set earlier, just as planned.

Taking a gun out of his pocket slowly and aiming it at Thirteen, Kuril was ready to win through dirty tactics. Taking one shot and missing, Thirteen took note that there was murderous intent behind Kuril's actions. Charging in zig-zags to avoid being hit by a bullet, Thirteen closed the gap between her and Kuril. Kuril landed a shot on her hip, to where she fell in front of him.

Kuril put the gun to her head, "I'm sorry for the awful life I gave you."

Thirteen remained still for a few seconds, Kuril's hand twitching. Thirteen took action quickly and jumped on him. Kuril, holding onto the gun, fired it into her at point-blank range. Her other hip, this time more to the stomach, was shot. Taking two bullet wounds was not easy, but Thirteen had no intention of losing to Kuril.

Grabbing Kuril's arm, she used her ability at last. Her other hand grabbed the gun and threw it across the dune. Burning through his shirt, Thirteen reached his skin in a single second. Burning that as well, Kuril reacted quickly to try and push her off him. Though it worked, Kuril was still on the ground, his right arm burnt up. Thirteen regained her balance quickly and pounced straight on Kuril, who was trying to stand up. Her hand burnt through his shirt again, reaching the skin of his chest. Burning that as well, Kuril's chest felt compacted. Thirteen's other hand reached down to his stomach and burnt it on a level beyond the other burns.

Standing over the two Violets was none other than Ten. "Not looking so hot, Kuril. That kind of hurts you know."

Kuril looked at Ten's arm and noticed a similar burn to his. He then blinked, making Ten's presence disappear. Kuril's body was under a lot of stress, and all he could do was try to push Mia off with the rest of his strength. He struggled a lot to push her off, but eventually got her to lose her positioning on his body, to where he kicked her off. Kuril pushed his body toward the gun, aiming directly at Thirteen and firing once. The bullet hit her directly in the right arm. She was barely getting up now too, and so was Kuril.

Thirteen got up and Kuril realized his Derringer was out of ammunition. The bullets shot were not of the most powerful gun, but the Derringer was a good enough gun for Kuril. The blond Violet found it in him to finally stand too. Their postures were showing signs of fatigue and readiness to fall down once their opponent does. Kuril's burns did a lot of stunning to his body as Thirteen's bullets weakened her speed and fighting capability. Thirteen and Kuril ran toward each other, hoping one punch could end the fight. At the last second, Thirteen pulled out a dagger and stabbed Kuril in his side.

Kuril's body grew limp, his head sunk below the shoulders of Thirteen. He tried grabbing onto Thirteen's shoulder for support. Thirteen stood there, embracing her victory, then removed the dagger and threw it away. Kuril fell to the ground face-first, Thirteen standing over him.

Silence was loud at the moment. Thirteen crouched on Kuril's back, ready to burn right through the back of his head and kill him. In a sudden turn of events, Kuril reached into his pocket and grabbed a dagger while not moving the rest of his body to disguise the fact he was able to move a little more. As Thirteen went to place her hand on Kuril's head, Kuril stabbed her as deep as he could into her side, removing the dagger immediately after digging into the wound with it. Thirteen fell next to Kuril in pain. Both of them had pride too large to even scream or yell in agony. They didn't want to show the pain they were in, but it was some of the worst physical pain they had felt in their lives.

The two bodies, wounded, one of them even burnt, laid next to each other. Kuril struggled to roll over to look at the sky, Thirteen already facing that direction. The sky was filled with clouds, little to no stars. Kuril eventually rolled over and took most of his remaining energy to face the skies above. The heaven above was almost pitch black, illuminated by the minimal stars. The clouds were a deep gray, floating by slowly. Time felt nonexistent.

"Can you move?" Kuril asked.

"Can you?"

"I can't."

"Got any tricks up your sleeve?" Thirteen went on with questions.

"You can't move either." Kuril sighed. "I guess we die here together."

"I'm satisfied with that." She relaxed her body. "I'm glad I could take your life."

"There's no one who I'd rather have kill me than you, Mia."

"Hey, Kuril." Mia looked over toward him.

Looking back, he responded, "What is it?"

"They didn't let me become the next head of the village because I was a girl, huh?"

"Yeah, it's messed up."

"The world won't give you things sometimes. We were born in a world where if you can't do this or you were born like that then you have no chance. Do you know how suffocating it felt for me?"

Kuril was silent.

"I want this world to burn for not giving me a chance," Mia spoke.

Kuril remained silent.

Mia's thoughts were leaving her mouth. "I want a world where we're all equal. A world where I would've been head of the Violet. A world where I wouldn't have been bullied in the only place I ever knew."

Kuril didn't speak.

"In the next life." Mia expressed her final emotions. "It'll be better."

The two remained silent. Twenty seconds passed.

"Rest easy, Mia."

Mia had already been unconscious for the last few seconds. Kuril was starting to see blues and couldn't focus. He tried to keep his eyes open, he wanted to live. Just one fighting chance was all Kuril wanted. His body grew weaker as he felt the numbness consume him. His body was slowly accepting his death, even though his mind didn't want the flame to die out. The two last Violets were next to each other, embracing each others' emotions. It was a beautiful tragedy, but Kuril knew he couldn't fight death. The end of the Violet was coming soon. Kuril's eyes closed on him, his breathing soothed, and he could no longer feel most of his body.

"In the next life."

CHAPTER V

"**H**ey, I think he's waking up!" a young adult woman hovered over a blond man, who was lying on an apartment couch.

The sound of sizzling and cracking was coming from the apartment kitchen, which radiated waves of heat. The woman was wearing a tanktop and shorts and clearly sweating in the heat.

"Where am I?" the blond man asked.

"We found you unconscious, bleeding out by one of my husband's colleagues. We took you in. You've been unconscious for a few days."

"I'm alive?" The blond man was clearly surprised, and he slowly moved to verify if it was true.

"Don't be too quick with moving around. I have a healing cloud, but I need you to be conscious in order for me to use it."

"Like those professional nurses for government officials?"

"Well, they're more talented than I am," she replied, "but I'm still good."

"Please fix me up."

"On it, captain!"

The woman took it in her to heal up the blond man on the couch, who occasionally yelped and showed signs of pain. It was only natural, as she had to apply pressure on the wounds to use her cloud. Kuril's body still was in pain, but the wounds were healed.

"I can't do much for the burn wounds. I did all I could, but the stab wound is completely fixed up. The burn wounds have been slightly healed, you might need to apply cream on them for a few days to properly heal," she said gleefully.

"Thank you, what's your name?"

"It's Amanda, and yours?"

"Kuril."

A man walked out of the kitchen in an apron. "Isn't that funny?"

"Who are you?" Kuril rose slightly from the couch.

"That's my husband, Robert!" Amanda introduced him.

Robert was a somewhat normal-sized guy, grayish-brown hair as well. His looks were normal. He looked like your average businessman. His suit was even worn inside his own house, but that was because he took pride in such an elegant outfit. His straight hair was short, and he didn't have much of it.

"It's Eleven to Kuril." Robert sighed.

"Robert, you helped save my life, though you already know I'm your enemy. Why is that?" Kuril couldn't process the idea in his head.

"We aren't enemies. I only work alongside Rose as an official member, not as a killer. I want to hear your story."

"I'm the last living member of the Violet."

"And you've come for revenge?"

"Exactly." Kuril was glad Robert got the memo. "That's all there is to it."

"Keep me out of it. Same with Amanda."

"How many people did you kill in the Rose raid?"

"I didn't even show up. I was against the idea." Robert sighed again.

"Your cloud is extraordinary I've heard, how does it contribute to Rose?"

"I'm sort of a morale booster, since I can get the members high in my individual world. I don't actually do much for the gang, I'm just in it so I can get cash for Amanda's sister."

"What's with her sister?" Kuril asked.

"She has to undergo cancer treatment. We can't afford luxuries. We have to do dirty deeds just to get by. I haven't killed anyone, but I'm sure as hell the biggest man in the drug industry right now. People pay just to go to my world."

"That's pretty interesting," Kuril said, standing up. "I should get going. How long was I asleep for?"

"Two days," Amanda said, "you looked like a little baby."

"Hey, shut it." Kuril let out a chuckle. "I couldn't help it."

"Won't you stay for lunch?" Robert offered.

Kuril sighed and opened the apartment door, "Unfortunately, I have to be going."

"I understand."

"Why are you so easygoing about me killing your members?" Kuril eyed Robert before leaving.

"It benefits me if they're gone. It benefits the world as well."

"So we have a truce?"

"If you'd like."

"I'll accept." Kuril started to close the door behind him. "Wait."

"What is it?"

Kuril's head pointed toward the ground as his words barely got out. "Is she alive?"

Robert and Amanda were silent, noticing the despair in his voice.

Kuril stopped the silence. "It's okay. I'll see you around."

Kuril left the apartment. During his exit, he left a drop of water on the door of the apartment to be wary of Eleven. Being spared so easily was a warning to Kuril that an ambush was coming.

Leaving the apartment building, the blond-haired Violet took a stroll on the street, walking toward the motel. It was about fifteen minutes away by foot, but Kuril didn't have money on him.

"Hey," Robert called out from behind Kuril, "you know I'm not done with you."

"I expected that. I'm only alive because of Amanda, and you wanted me dead all along. Am I right?" Kuril turned around.

Robert had a tendency to sigh a lot. "Spot on."

"You wish to fight?"

A drop of water fell from Kuril's hand.

"Let's take it to that one empty lot by Zipline."

"Sure, why not?" The blond-haired man quickly followed the well-dressed Rose member ahead of him.

The two men walked toward the Zipline bar, which wasn't very far. Both of them had no idea that Nine died in that exact lot. Kuril had no idea if Junil was safe, as Robert had no idea of any casualties since Fourteen's death, similar to the other Rose members.

The city was somewhat quiet that night, likely because it was a little after rush hour. You could hear the occasional cat on the road and the angered businessman on the phone, but there weren't crowds of people.

Kuril already had a plan in mind to defeat Robert, and it was quite simple. Robert had no idea of Kuril's cloud or even if he had one. Though Robert expected Kuril to have a cloud, he wasn't certain. Preparing for the worst so he could outshine Kuril, Robert was strategizing the fight in his own head. His confidence in his own cloud wasn't very big, despite being one of the most powerful clouds Rose has ever seen.

"We're here." Robert headed to one end of the empty lot.

The empty lot didn't have Nine's body, as it was already disposed of by the time Kuril woke up. Kuril walked over to the other end of the empty lot. If the worst came up, he'd just reform himself at the apartment door.

"Let's get this going." Robert cracked his knuckles.

Kuril stood still. "Come at me."

A giant portal opened under Kuril, to which Kuril dodged as if he knew it was coming.

"You know my cloud?" Robert was confused.

"I have a spy on my side." Kuril got back on his feet. "They didn't inform me that you'd resort to cheap tricks."

"I just feel like winning quickly, since it's inevitable."

"We'll see about that."

Kuril charged at Robert, who defended himself by creating a portal in front of Kuril. Kuril stopped in his tracks, almost entering Robert's portal. Entering Robert's own world would be the worst for Kuril, so he had to avoid it at all costs.

Robert's self-satisfied expression grew more obvious as Kuril grew frustrated. "Can't hit me?"

"Your cloud is very impressive."

Kuril tried going around the portal, strifing to his left, but was met with another portal. The other portal was withdrawn, which confirmed one thing for Kuril: there could only be one portal at a time.

The Violet took another shot and ran toward Robert, who summoned the portal in front of him again. Strifing to his right, then faking Robert out and going to his left, Kuril managed to get close to Robert.

Tackling Robert to the ground, Kuril started to punch him in the face. At this point, Kuril's cloud was still anonymous to Robert. Robert's face kept going left and right taking blow after blow.

Robert managed to grab Kuril's fists and restrict his arms for a few seconds before letting out a witty line. "I've won."

A portal opened beneath the both of them, dragging the two fighters to Robert's world.

"Isn't it wonderful?" Robert let out a smile.

The world showcased was a realm full of illusions. It felt almost like Kuril was tripping on drugs. The fear of what would happen to him made Kuril shiver. All around Robert's dimension was a combination of things that didn't match. It was odd. The world around the two didn't have any application to physics whatsoever, eliminating all gravity and the laws that came with it.

"I hope you enjoy dying in flames for what you did to my comrades." Robert laughed as the world around him became almost demonic.

Kuril ran off into a forest that was crawling with giant bugs. It wasn't very easy to get around, but he had to make sure he got out of Robert's line of sight. Robert, who was focused on creating the Hell-like conditions for Kuril, didn't notice he got away. Kuril ran across the forest, dodging giant creatures as he found himself trapped in a dimension that seemed like a never-ending torture chamber.

"You can't run, I can just bring you back to me!" Robert said, laughing.

Robert attempted to bring Kuril back to him through teleportation, but nothing happened. Robert's expression changed dramatically, realizing his ability was failing on him.

"Kuril! Where the fuck are you?"

Robert got serious very quickly, his expression returning to normal. Out of nowhere, the entire world became a climate that resembled Hell. There were cliffs with lava, there was fire, and there was smoke in the air. The cracking ground and red sky complimented each other as every piece of Robert's dimension became a no man's land.

"You'll die here, then!" Robert's voice quickly changed to anger.

Robert left his world in order to not pass out from the heat. He was going to leave Kuril to die.

"Excuse me, Amanda?" Kuril called from outside the apartment door, knocking twice.

The door opened. "Welcome back, Kuril!"

"Thank you! Can I stay here for a few minutes?"

"Sure!" Amanda was glad to see her guest return.

"Do you have a gun I can borrow?" Kuril asked.

"A gun?" Amanda asked.

"Someone is going to enter this apartment very soon and try to kill me. Take cover and you'll be fine."

"I don't know if my insurance covers—"

"I'll cover it. Don't worry, Amanda. I'll protect you with my life and that includes the apartment you saved me in."

Amanda's eyes glowed seeing how courageous Kuril was. In reality, Kuril was bluffing. He actually plotted something that would be an awful sight for Amanda. The apartment door closed behind Kuril, and Amanda handed Kuril the gun that she kept for self-defense.

"How many shots in one round?" Kuril asked.

"Six."

"Should be enough." Kuril got on one knee and aimed directly at the door. "Look away and hide."

"S-Sure." Amanda felt a lump in her throat, clearly oblivious to the situation at hand.

This was exactly Kuril's plan: go to Robert's world and return to the apartment using his cloud that he hid from Robert.

The door was shut. Kuril was still aiming, ready to fire six bullets straight into Robert's head when he returned to the apartment. Amanda had no idea Robert was the enemy. Time was standing still as Kuril and Amanda stayed frozen in their respective spots.

"Who's after you?" Amanda asked, breaking the silence.

"A criminal."

"Okay."

The doorknob shifted, Kuril's grip tightened, and Amanda started to shake. Hiding behind some furniture, she didn't answer the following knocks. The man at the door waited for Amanda to open it for him, but she didn't move from her spot. Amanda was curled in a ball, scared for her life.

Outside the apartment door, keys started to rattle, and the doorknob shifted once again. The door finally peaked open.

"I'm home—"

Three cracks fired straight at the open door. The man fell back, unable to move. Kuril got up and shot him three more times in where he assumed his heart was to make sure he couldn't be saved by his own world or Amanda.

"He's dead." Kuril tossed the gun away.

Amanda got up and saw her husband dead on the floor. Her face grew purple, her legs started to shake, and she eventually hit the floor. On all fours, she crawled toward Eleven.

Kuril walked toward the body. "If you try to save him, I'll kill you too."

"Why?!" Amanda screamed, her beauty now tarnished by her own emotions.

Amanda's head was bulging, her vision was spinning. Teardrops fell to the floor as her heart tightened. Everything felt cold and fake. As Amanda crawled over and reached out to touch Robert's bloody head, a teardrop fell on his face. At this point, Amanda started uncontrollably shaking and crying.

"Why?" Amanda exploded.

"He had to die."

Uncontrollable screams came from the voice of the woman who saved Kuril's life. The despair overwhelming her, the pain filling her, and the anguish taking over. The screams were beginning to break. Kuril's face remained the same. He couldn't feel any sense of care. Amanda's body continued to tremble, her heart racing in the heat of the moment.

"Why?!"

"Affiliation with Rose is guilt."

Amanda was silent, unable to process the memories all thrown away by six simple bullets in one moment. Her husband, who she dearly loved, was gone. The future was gone. There was nothing more for Robert and Amanda.

"Now you can feel a portion of my despair."

"You're a monster," Amanda cried. "You're a fucking monster!"

Kuril let his arm transform into water and manipulated the fluid to surround Amanda's head, enclosing her neck and head in a bubble. "Would you repeat that for me?"

Amanda was drowning, unable to shake out of the bubble of water. Whenever she moved her head, the water came with it. She couldn't breathe.

"I'm asking you to repeat yourself," Kuril said, watching her struggle to hold onto her life. His eyes showed how he felt: nonchalant. He disintegrated the water and reformed his arm, releasing Amanda from the bubble of water he imprisoned her in.

Amanda caught her breath. "You're a—"

She tried to repeat herself, but was met with a kick straight to the face, sending her to the floor.

Kuril towered over Robert's wife. "I don't think I quite heard you."

Amanda laid on the ground, almost stunned from her emotional turmoil and the beatdown she was receiving.

Kuril walked over and looked down on her, making sure they locked eyes. "Repeat yourself or I'll end your life, you dirty-handed fucking bitch."

Amanda opened her mouth, but nothing came out.

Kuril sent another kick straight to her temple. "You're so fucking pathetic."

"Why…?"

"You affiliate with Rose."

Amanda didn't refute him. "Kill me…"

"Repent for your sins in Hell, where Robert burns endlessly. Until the end of time, you will be nothing except flesh and meat roasting in the fiery pits below." Kuril's arm transformed back into water.

The water manipulated itself into a sphere-like shape, only connected to Kuril's body by a thread of water. The water encompassed Amanda, who let herself die to Kuril's hand.

"You shouldn't have saved me."

After two minutes of just keeping the same position, Amanda was surely dead. While it takes around one minute for an adult to drown, Kuril didn't take his chances. Here he had two bodies: Eleven and his love. Turning his arm back to normal, he walked over Robert's body, which was in and out of the apartment, and spit on it.

"What a mess," Ten spoke from the back of the apartment, coming out of the kitchen.

"Ten."

"Kuril."

"So you can talk to me?" Kuril asked.

"Can I?"

"Seems so."

Ten chuckled. "You're really wreaking havoc for Rose. You seem scary."

"What the fuck is your cloud? Aren't you dead?"

"I don't need a body to be alive."

The Violet stared at Ten. "What do you mean?"

"I can stay alive and exist... by living in someone's mind."

Kuril walked up to Ten and grabbed his hand. "You are touchable. That's one thing."

"I will always be human."

"No one else can see you."

"Good observation."

Kuril looked away for a second. "You can't teleport or be anywhere else until you're out of my sight, correct?"

"Maybe, maybe not."

Kuril liquified his arm and sent water up Ten's nostrils and into his lungs. "We'll see then."

"Okay, okay, you're right!"

Kuril reformed his arm. "So you can't do anything in my line of sight."

"I cannot do anything when I am in your line of sight. I am like a ghost basically."

"You're a ghost and your actions are dependent on mine?"

"Correct."

Kuril slapped himself. "Did you feel that?"

"No."

"How do I make you leave me alone?"

Ten looked into Kuril's eyes. "Why should I tell you that?"

"So be it." Kuril turned away.

Kuril walked out of the apartment, not caring about a simple thing that just happened. Kuril lacked empathy for his enemies on high levels. Footsteps echoed through the hallway of the apartment building hall. He walked out of the building, but with his hands stained from the blood of his enemies.

Continuing back on his path to the motel, Kuril took his phone out and called Junil.

"Kuril, you're alright?" Junil immediately asked.

"Of course. I just got rid of Thirteen and Eleven."

"Do you need me to pick you up?"

"I'm walking back to the motel. Any news?"

"I eliminated Nine. The chess board is in our control."

"Don't get cocky," Kuril kept walking the streets of Velindas. "You only need two pieces to checkmate most of the time."

"I'll catch you at the motel then."

Junil hung up on Kuril. Shrugging it off, Kuril continued to walk that same path that he was taking earlier. The motel was still fifteen minutes away, but those fifteen minutes were going to be some of the longest for Kuril.

"Good morning, sleepyhead."

Thirteen woke up to Three hovering right over her. As she jolted up, Three flung his neck back in order to not collide heads with

Thirteen. Yelping in pain from the sudden movement, Thirteen held onto her wounds as she slowly observed her surroundings.

"Three…"

"Don't move so quickly," William sat down on the back of a church pew to face Thirteen, who was supposed to be laying down on the one behind where William was sitting.

"You killed Twelve."

"Is that so?"

"You think I'm fucking stupid?"

"You must've overheard us," William replied.

"What the fuck did you do to her?"

Thirteen yelped once again in pain as her anger caused her to try pressuring William. Swooping his black hair back, he chuckled as Thirteen's face started to fill with malice. As the church doors opened, Thirteen looked back as Kyra entered the building.

"Kyra?" Thirteen's eyes started to water.

"Mia," Kyra replied.

"How are you alive?"

"I faked my death. I'm okay."

Standing up slowly, Mia walked over to Kyra, who stood there waiting for her. Hugging Kyra, the Violet girl started to cry as she felt the touch of the girl she never thought she would see again. Tears soaked onto Kyra's clothes as William watched the two reunite.

"Why?"

Kyra put her hand on Mia's hair as she brushed it slowly, letting Mia cry. "I had to. I needed to end my affiliation with Rose in order to help Three investigate."

"Just call me William," he shouted from across the church.

"I'm sorry," Kyra continued.

"I'm just so happy."

"Me too. I was worried sick about you, even though William and I planned on saving your life either way."

"Please don't ever go away again, Kyra."

"I won't."

"Well." William put his hand up to signal he was speaking. "Nice reunion, but Mia is now also no longer affiliated with Rose! You're deemed dead, Violet girl."

Mia stood up straight and wiped her eyes, looking over at the mastermind in the back. "Was this your plan, William?"

"It was."

"What did you hope to achieve by making me suspicious of you?"

William cracked his knuckles. "I was testing your loyalty. I wanted to know whether you were more loyal to Rose as an organization or Rose as people. Better yet, I found out you were just loyal to Kyra."

"The conversation between you two was staged?"

"It was."

"This makes me a member of your investigative squad?" Mia asked.

"It does!" William chuckled. "You catch on quickly."

Mia replied, "What exactly are we investigating?"

"A little plan One and Two have."

Mia raised an eyebrow. "A plan?"

"The Blooming Day."

CHAPTER VI

A day after the town of Norman was burnt, Adam got away with the brother and sister duo of James and Kaylin. They hid in several areas, though there were no leads to their guilt due to the stealth. Kaylin was safe from the fire as it happened, and Adam and James left no trails or witnesses. Almost everyone belonging to the small neighborhood or nearby ones in Norman were victims to that duo.

In an abandoned grocery store by the edge of Norman, Kaylin napped on the ground. She was very tired from the stress and pain of listening to the tragedy of Norman, but Adam and James were wide awake and relaxing while planning their next move.

"It didn't work, Adam."

"What more can we do?"

James punched a wall in the abandoned store they were hiding in. "I don't fucking know!"

"Calm down." Adam looked over at Kaylin, who was sleeping

on James' oversized coat instead of the dirty floor. "You might wake her."

"I don't get it, Adam. I killed her parents, I set her fucking neighborhood on fire. I had to suffer as I did all of that! I just fucking suffer all the time! Why can't I just get what I want?"

Adam kept his eyes on Kaylin to make sure she was still asleep. "Quiet."

James looked at his palm. "I need to do more. I can't go back to who I used to be."

"What's this mentality, James?"

"Someone must cause suffering, whether it's on others or themselves. I was born for that role. Why else would I have such a terrorizing cloud?"

Kaylin spoke up, having heard most of the conversation after James accidentally woke her up. "You were not made to bring suffering."

"Kaylin, how much did you hear?" Adam's eyes widened as he looked over at the fragile girl.

"What is it you want, James?"

"Shut up," James said, looking over at Kaylin with an awfully condescending look. "You have no idea the shit I do for you. You have no idea how I feel."

"What reward do you get from killing our parents?"

"You have it so easy. Keep your mouth shut."

Adam looked into James' eyes and saw what he felt. He was tired, but not sleepy. He was frustrated, but not angry. He was growing worse mentally everyday, and there was nothing anyone could do. James had intentions of stepping over even more lines simply because he didn't want to be pulled back into reality.

James took notice of Adam looking at him. "What do you want?"

"Calm down a little, James. She's clueless to all of this and there is nothing you can do about it."

"I want to show her how I feel."

"The Blooming Day will never work then."

James gave that same condescending look to Adam. "Then tell me, how can we ever make it work?"

Adam signalled James to leave the area so they could discuss it privately. "We're headed out, Kaylin."

James looked at Kaylin as if to give a light goodbye, but he saw tears. Kaylin was crying, and James' face went pale. He slowly walked over to her.

"I'm sorry, Kaylin—"

"You're a monster!" she screamed.

Adam watched the scene. James slowly backed up, and all Adam saw was his breaking face. James was about to cry, but he knew he had to be strong in front of Kaylin. A tear or two fell, but you couldn't tell he was crying.

James' voice sounded completely normal. "I'm sorry."

"Does an apology bring back the life you stole from me?" she yelled.

"It doesn't."

"So be quiet! I don't want to hear from you at all!"

Kaylin's words put an end to James' voice. He started to walk outside and signalled Adam to follow him. They were going to discuss the Blooming Day plan. James felt soulless, impure, stripped, and ugly. He felt like the worst human on the face of the planet, even if he thought he was doing the right thing. It was going to be okay though, because James felt like he had his plan set in stone: the Blooming Day.

"Before Adam and I go out, I want to give you something to defend yourself with."

James walked back toward Kaylin and reached his hand out, giving a closed switchblade. He grabbed Kaylin's hand gently and directed it to the switchblade.

"Use this for emergencies only."

Kaylin nodded.

James turned back around. "I'll be back soon."

"James."

"What is it?"

Kaylin went silent. "I don't know."

James walked away.

Back at Rose's hideout, a meeting was being hosted by James. Usually meetings are hosted every now and then for when the gang wants to do something, but they're also for emergencies. Everyone in the meeting knew how the current meeting was about the loss of Rose's members and how to stop it.

A man in a blazer took a cigarette out of his pocket. "So why are several members missing from an urgent meeting, One?" he asked.

"You may notice only eight of us are present." James started the meeting. "The other seven, which were all lower levels, have died."

The man in the blazer threw his cigarette to the ground. "You're kidding, right?"

James' face was empty of expression and rather calm. "I'm not, Three. Kaylin has been kidnapped as well."

"So, final eight members?" Three folded his arms.

"It seems that way." Adam tried to get more involvement from the other members. "You might be next, Eight."

"I'm not a fighter, but I believe if I could combine with someone else's cloud, then we may have a fighting chance." Eight put his finger to his chin as if he was thinking.

"I could definitely use your cloud." Six's booming voice made a presence.

Eight looked over at Six. "Nobody even knows your cloud's ability, Six."

"The ability to control someone based on fear. The more frightened someone is, the more control I can take over their body." Six revealed his cloud's true ability. "By knowing their positions through walls, I can control them one by one and stun them, to which we can just shoot them down."

"Impressive, Six. I'll take you up on that," Eight reached agreement to combine with Six to take out Kuril and Junil.

"You said Kaylin was abducted, One?" Six asked.

"Yes," James responded.

"That means her charm is likely already in place."

"What do you mean?" Adam asked.

"If they're all on good terms with each other, they should feel fear for each other's lives as both friends and fighters."

"I seem to understand." Adam felt the pieces coming together like a puzzle.

"In order for this to go through, we need to have distractions."

"You're saying we have to lure them out and separate them?" Adam asked.

"That's the idea. I want to aim for the detective first, so we have to bait the other one out."

"I can handle that," Adam confidently spoke.

"Tomorrow afternoon." Six's plan was unbeatable if executed perfectly. "Eight and I will scout their hideout and move in peacefully in order to deceive that detective. On the other hand, Two will lure out the other one and distract him before he can return to the hideout."

"Understood," Adam was ready.

"Let's finish this war," Eight said.

"Twelve's final wish to hand down the location they were hiding out at came in perfectly. It's time to win for her." Six's presence was the largest in the room.

Confidence was booming through the room. The war could end if everything worked perfectly. Junil and Kuril eliminated, Kaylin retrieved. The chess board had minimal pieces for Rose, but had a gambit that couldn't fail.

Meanwhile at the motel, it was late at night. Kuril had finally arrived at the scene, opened the door to his dusty motel room and was greeted with the same two beds. The scene had not shifted at all since he rented the room, excluding a few mugs. The only real difference was Junil and Kaylin's presence.

"I'm back." Kuril closed the door behind him.

Kuril was met with a big surprise, seeing Kaylin walking with Junil directing her by holding her shoulders.

"Welcome back," Kaylin said, walking a little faster than her previous pace.

"Hey, don't get antsy!" Junil was trying to keep up with Kaylin.

"I see you and Junil have spent some time while I was out," Kuril said, walking toward Kaylin. "Did you two think I died?"

"I wouldn't be surprised," Junil replied.

"That's not fair." Kuril sighed and moved to his chair he sat in during the day.

"I... was really scared," Kaylin muttered.

Kuril's good hearing picked up on her words, to which he lightheartedly chuckled. "I'm fine."

"No love for the Phantom of Velindas? Come on, Kaylin—"

"I was worried about you too, Junil!" Kaylin's voice bursted like a bubble and the room went silent.

"I was just kidding, Kaylin. Do you really think the Phantom of Velindas could lose a fight?" Junil's rhetorical question disregarded entirely how Kaylin felt.

"Thank you, Kaylin." Kuril looked at Junil. "Your concern reminds me that there are people who really care for me."

"You should jot it in your head that I never lose," Junil stated, "but I appreciate your humanity more than I say I do."

"I apologize," Kaylin replied.

"There's no need." The detective sent his eyes toward Kuril.

"What is it, Junil?" Kuril asked.

"How was the fighting? Two people must've been tough." Junil scratched his head.

"It was fine and all went smoothly." He wasn't very big on his words.

"As for me, Nine was a breeze, but I was cocky and took two hits. I got to the hospital and a healing cloud controlled it from there. I got out of that hospital and we've been waiting for you for about a day."

Kuril took a look at Kaylin, ignoring the topic at hand. "How blind are you?"

"I'm unable to see completely."

"When did this happen?"

"I was born like this."

"How old is James?"

"He's 25."

"That's around four years older than the both of us, three above Junil."

"He founded Rose as a teenager. The raid on the Violet happened when he was just sixteen." Kaylin started to fidget her hands.

"Was James always this way?"

Kaylin's face was growing pale. "It started when our parents…"

"Hey! Don't push it!" Junil grabbed her shoulders and directed her to the bed, where she sat down.

"Are you alright?" Kuril asked.

"I'm fine…" Kaylin responded.

"If you can explain this story to me, I'd like to hear it."

"When we were children, our parents passed." Kaylin was starting to get a grip on herself and her emotions.

"What happened?"

"James killed our father. I was twelve at the time."

"Why would he do that?"

"I have no idea. When our mother walked in, she saw her husband dead and started to break. She screamed, making James kill her too in the heat of the moment."

"Was he trying to hide his tracks?"

"He told me that he didn't want the neighbors to find out," Kaylin answered. "The rest of the story is from my memory."

"Go on."

"I walked in, naive and happy. According to James, this was about fifteen minutes after the murder."

"So you never heard your mother scream?" Kuril asked.

"I wasn't near the house at the time."

"If I'm allowed to: how were they killed?"

"Both were stabbed in vital points repeatedly to make sure they stayed down without a sound."

"I'm sorry to hear. What happened when you came in?"

"I thought I was home alone, then I heard breathing. I went on to ask who it was that was breathing, and then James told me... he killed them."

"What did he sound like?"

"His voice was practically breaking. I could tell he was on the verge of mentally snapping. He was about to cry."

"Pause." Junil looked over at Kuril. "Why would James cry? He's one of the most ruthless killers out there."

"He was such an innocent kid before that incident," Kaylin answered, "that was the first time he took someone's life.

"But why would he kill his parents? Was it self-defense?"

"Our parents never laid their hands on us, but I have no other idea why he would've killed our parents."

"What happened after?" Kuril interrupted.

"I heard something hit the ground, likely the knife he used," Kaylin responded, "then he hugged me and told me how much he loved me."

"What was that like?" Kuril continued his questioning.

"His voice was that of someone who was sobbing. I heard crying mixed with the heart of a man who realized he would never be pure again."

"Anything else?"

"He told me that he would never let me go. He told me that he'd do anything for me. He even told me that he had to do this."

"He had to kill your parents?" Junil jumped in again.

"The story I just told was a mixture of both of our perspectives, since I was late to the scene and unable to see anything."

"Why would he have to kill your parents?" Junil started to look at the ceiling.

"I don't know."

"What happened when Rose was founded?" Kuril asked.

"When Rose was founded, James and Adam were the only two members. I met Adam the same day Rose had their opening ceremony."

"Opening ceremony?"

"James and Adam burnt down as many houses as they could by the neighborhood James and I lived in."

"When was this?"

"Two days after my parents died."

"You were twelve, correct?" Junil asked.

"Yes, and James was sixteen."

"Adam is a year older than me, so he was likely fifteen. A few days before he turned thirteen, he left the orphanage."

"Why?" Kaylin asked.

"It's not a story for you, but I'm not surprised he came across James on his journey. The two are magnetic. They're deadly and mysterious."

"Can I add something?" Kaylin started to fidget again.

"Go ahead," Kuril replied.

"Rose has a plan called the Blooming Day."

"What is it?" Kuril asked.

"I have no idea."

"When is it?"

"Now that Rose is dwindling in numbers, it might be soon."

Kuril sighed and looked at Junil, who was also clueless. The room was filled with questioning silence. The two men were pondering and exchanging glances, but Kaylin was just staring into nothingness like always. She had no idea why the room was so quiet.

Kaylin tried to break the silence. "We should keep an eye out for whatever the Blooming—"

Junil's phone rang.

"I should take that." Junil took his phone out. "It's Adam."

Junil looked at Kuril and then answered the call.

"Hey, Junil. Scheduled fight, Kuril and I!" Adam's words sent shock to Junil. He had no one he wanted to win that fight, but if both lost, it would be even worse.

"When?" Junil replied.

"Right now by Kibbler Street. Tell Kuril to meet me there now."

Adam hung up on the phone. Junil placed the phone back in his pocket and looked at Kuril. The Violet read the detective very easily: a fight was going to happen again.

"Kibbler Street, it's Two."

"Then I have to go."

Kaylin's expression returned to that of one who was suffering from neutrality. She knew that Two was way out of Kuril's league. Two was a one of a kind man.

"Please be safe, Kuril," Kaylin said.

"I will."

The Violet opened the motel door and left the scene, leaving Junil and Kaylin alone again. The room was filled with silence again, but the two had the same mindset: Kuril couldn't win this fight. Junil had practically sent Kuril to his death.

"Why didn't you tell him?" Kaylin asked.

Junil was silent.

Kuril walked down to Kibbler Street, only a few minutes away by foot. Not knowing what Adam looked like, Kuril just relaxed by a streetlight that was next to a bike rack.

"Kuril." A tan man greeted the Violet in front of him. His red glasses were very noticeable.

"Are you Two?"

"Of course. Let's move to a more isolated spot."

"Seems like a good idea," Kuril replied.

"By the way, we're going to make a few stops before we get to the empty space."

Back at the motel, Junil and Kaylin sat there in silence. Outside of the motel, Eight was scanning the room.

"Is your headset connected?" Eight asked into his earphones.

"I got it," Six responded, standing out by the motel.

"You won't need to break in, the door is unlocked," Eight said, scanning the inside of the room with his cloud's ability to see through walls.

"Is that because Kuril just left?"

"Yeah."

"When should I go in?"

"When Junil uses the bathroom, then follow the plan accordingly."

"Understood."

The headset that Six wore was suspicious, but no one was around that motel at the moment anyways. As for Eight, being behind the motel was a good hiding spot for him. Adam was on the other side of Velindas distracting Kuril. The plan was going as they wanted.

"Junil is using the bathroom, go in now!" Eight commanded through the headset.

Six opened the motel room door at a normal volume as to not startle Junil, then rushed in for Kaylin. Taking out a pistol with a silencer, Six aimed directly at Kaylin, who had no idea who was there. Firing a gunshot into Kaylin's leg, Six grabbed Kaylin and held her in a hostage-like spot. She started to scream in pain, which was answered by the bathroom door opening.

"Stop!" Junil rushed out of the bathroom.

The sight that awaited him was one of blood. Kaylin's leg had a bullet in it, and she was very sensitive to the pain. She pressed her teeth together and tried to endure the pain.

"Get on your knees, Junil, or she dies," Six demanded.

Junil got on his knees as Six demanded.

"Not so powerful now, Phantom of Velindas," Six joked.

Junil remained silent so as to not anger him. Seeing his unpleasant reaction, Six fired another bullet into Kaylin, this time in her leg.

"Kaylin!" Junil screamed.

Six let out a laugh. "That's all I needed."

The chess match was in Six's favor for one reason: Junil and Kaylin had no idea he was coming and had no idea what his cloud did. Six was a smart fighter, despite his cockiness and short temper.

Six's cloud, the ability to control people based on the amount of fear they're feeling, took control of Junil. He was unable to move. Junil knew this would be the end of the war. Kuril was fighting an unbeatable opponent and Junil and Kaylin were now in the hands of their enemy.

"Six takes another win." The Rose member celebrated his victory.

A silhouette appeared in the doorway of the motel room. It was a slender man in a dark purple jacket that dropped to his waists. His arrival looked biblical. The sunset behind him, the perfect timing, the way he looked in that doorway. He looked like an angel coming from the Heavens to deliver a message from God. His black pants and white shirt showed that he was no angel, but rather, a human being. The dark purple coat almost blended in with his mundane clothing.

"I'm sorry I was late," James said, taking his first footsteps into the motel room.

"One, I did it! Once Kuril returns, this war is over!" Six's excitement was overbearing for James.

Followed by James was William, the third highest rank of Rose. "My, my. Isn't that just nice?"

"Three? Look! I ended the war!"

William smiled with closed eyes. "Good job."

"Can I see that pistol of yours?" James asked.

"Why?"

"I want to shoot Junil."

"Go for it, this is your gang."

James grabbed the pistol out of Six's hands and observed it. "Who were you working with?" he asked.

"Eight." Six placed Kaylin down on the bed and stretched.

"Where is he?"

"Look outside the window."

James opened the window blinds and saw Eight with another headset. It was apparent that Eight was connected to Six's headset through the other headset, where Eight gave directions.

"Can Eight hear you through that?" James asked.

"Yeah."

"Can you tell him to come here?"

"Hey, Eight. One wants you to come here," Eight said into his headset.

Through the motel door was Eight, immediately scanning the room to see a stunned Junil and a bleeding Kaylin. One's daring eyes shined the most in the room. Eight's tall physique was outmatched by One, who was a little over six feet tall. Six was smiling, accomplishing something most Rose members couldn't.

"Let's celebrate, Eight!" Six's genuine smile was not a common occurrence.

"This is a nice pistol," James said, "where did you get it?"

"I think I got—"

Two shots were fired into Six's head, his brain matter spilling onto the motel wall behind him.

"What the hell?" Eight's face grew pale as he backed up.

Two more shots were fired, this time into Eight's head. His body fell onto the floor, blood reaching almost to the motel room door.

William's smile didn't fade. "What a shame."

Junil's body immediately eased up after Six's death.

"Fucking idiots! You can't do a single thing right!" James yelled.

"You shot your own members?" Junil asked James, getting on his own two feet.

"They hurt Kaylin."

"Her safety is enough for you to kill your own members?"

James eased up. "Of course."

"Should I contact medical assistance then?"

"Please."

Junil took out his phone and contacted medics. It was beyond his own mind to see him working with One, but Kaylin's safety was a priority to him too.

"Are you alright, Kaylin?" James asked, doing what he could to ease the bleeding.

James elevated Kaylin's legs, but he didn't know much else in terms of stopping bleeding. It was ironic that one of the most notorious people alive didn't know how to prevent or slow bleeding at all.

"It hurts, James," Kaylin cried out, "it hurts really bad."

"It's okay, I'm here for you. Please just hold on."

"Medical assistance is on the way, Kaylin," Junil told the girl, who was lying on his bloodied bed.

"Pain is temporary, Kaylin." James' eyes were tearing up. "Please just get through it."

"Why are you tearing up?" Junil asked.

"I can't stand to see her in pain. I never want to see her like this."

"I can understand that."

"Are you the Phantom of Velindas I keep hearing about?" James asked.

"That's me."

"You're a good person." James was smiling, though his eyes were flooding with tears.

"You should get out of here. I'll take care of Kaylin."

"Thank you, Junil." James wiped his tears and looked at him.

William cleared his throat. "I'm fully capable of taking care of Kaylin, One. Should I get rid of Junil while we can?"

"No, that won't be necessary."

"Oh, really?"

"We'll meet him again later. Let's be on our way."

James' angelic presence left the room. As James left the room, William followed him, almost as if he were a bodyguard. A cloud of mystery was left behind. Two bodies were in the room, both

Rose members. James' leaving changed the temperature of the room, making Junil able to relax without the pressure.

Hearing the ambulance outside, Junil grabbed Kaylin. She had passed out from the pain. The detective carried her outside and to the ambulance, where they laid her down.

"She was shot in both legs, nowhere fatal for her walking abilities in the future," Junil said.

"We'll take care of her," one of the medical experts said.

They were all gone as soon as they came.

On the other side of Velindas, Adam and Kuril were eating out. It was a normal dinner, yet the lackadaisical attitude of Kuril made the Violet drop his walls. He was just eating out, waiting for anything Adam would initiate. Adam didn't each much, which was surprising to Kuril, who assumed by Adam's build that he would eat more. Instead, Adam had a salad with a Martini, which was a strange combination.

"How's the food?" Adam gave Kuril a smile.

"It's great, but will we ever fight?"

Adam's phone rang. Immediately picking it up, Adam heard the man on the line.

"Yes, James. I was supposed to be a distraction for Eight and Six. What did they do?" Adam asked.

It hit Kuril hard: he was just being distracted. The real scene was at the motel.

Kuril rose from his chair and slammed the table. "What happened?"

"It's all settled now?" Adam asked, not caring about Kuril. "So I can go back?"

Kuril waited for his turn.

"Thanks. Is Junil okay? How about Kaylin?"

Kuril listened in.

"I can't believe they were both killed! I'll call you later."

Adam hung up. Kuril's face was stuck. Kuril wasn't moving. All Kuril could do was stare into Adam's eyes with an expression of shock and hatred. The darkness took over Kuril's expression as his mind ran.

"I'm kidding. Junil and Kaylin are fine. Kaylin is injured and being treated, while Junil is unharmed. Both Eight and Six are dead."

"You say that like you don't care."

"I don't care."

"You don't care if your own comrades die?"

"They're pawns." Adam let out a sigh and signaled the waiter to provide a bill for the food.

"You're ruthless."

"I'm just nuclear."

"What does that even mean?" Kuril asked.

"No idea."

"Can I ask you a question?"

"Hit me with it."

"What is the Blooming Day?"

Adam paused for a few seconds, then smiled. "It's the day Rose's wishes come true."

"Elaborate."

"Tomorrow. I think."

"It's only the final five and Seven now, am I correct?"

"Seven killed himself."

Kuril was surprised, but it was a welcome surprise.

"Any reason?" Kuril asked.

"Didn't want to do life anymore. He hated it the minute he joined Rose and I guess this situation was the final nail in his coffin."

Adam got the check and placed a load of cash in it. He signaled the waiter back immediately to get the check. Adam wanted to get out of there fast. He was bored.

"My opponent is Junil," Adam said.

"Mine is James."

"Then let's keep it that way."

"You're still my enemy, but it's Junil's job."

"Sounds about right."

Adam stood up and left. Kuril got up as well and followed him. Reaching the restaurant exit, the two parted ways. There were no more words to be said, but their minds were running.

On his walk back to the motel, Kuril heard a voice from the alleyway. "Hello!"

"What do you want, Ten?"

"I'm going to keep bothering you."

"You're annoying. Leave me alone."

Ten sighed. "You know, Kuril, you need to lighten up."

Kuril walked into the alleyway. He was clearly not up for the shenanigans of Ten right now. Kuril punched Ten out of frustration, yet he felt the hit too. Kuril was struck by realization, and immediately pieced together Ten's ability.

"Ten, did you lie about not feeling my slap back in Eleven's apartment?"

Ten didn't respond. In turn, Kuril formed a liquid bubble using his arm and pinned Ten to the wall. Kuril felt his own back as Ten's spine hit the wall. It all made sense: Ten's ghostlike cloud, which existed after death, could replicate pain onto whoever he chose.

"Wait a minute," Ten said.

"Fuck off."

Kuril took a deep breath and wrapped Ten's head in the bubble of water, rendering both of them unable to breathe. Kuril didn't take his eyes off Ten, who was struggling to gasp for air. Kuril's chest felt cramped as his mind screamed that he needed air. His heart rate fluctuated as Ten continued to struggle even more. Looking at Kuril, he saw eyes that were not moving and not even close to blinking. The eyelids didn't twitch at all. In front of Ten, there was a man more ghostlike than him. Ten closed his eyes and stopped struggling, but Kuril didn't remove the bubble until he knew he had to breathe. He removed the bubble and gasped for air as Ten's body hit the floor.

Both of the men tried to catch their breath, clenching onto their shirts with each shortened breath. Looking at each other, Ten put his hand up. Looking down, he dropped his hand to relax his body.

"Kuril, we need to talk," Ten said, breathing heavily.

"About?"

"Rose."

Kuril swallowed and continued to breathe heavily until he was okay enough to converse with Ten. "What about Rose?"

"Not all of us were"—Ten breathed in and relaxed as he had finally caught his breath— "there on the day of your people's massacre."

Kuril's eyes widened. "Who was?"

"One told us that he didn't want us to carry the burden of murder, so he would do it himself alongside Two, Three, and Thirteen. Twelve followed Thirteen along." Ten coughed. "I think they're lovers or something."

"The burden of murder?"

"We're a bunch of thieves, yet we all have the capability to kill. I tell you what happened before the massacre because Rose seems fishy. I don't like it. I don't even want to be in Rose, I just need money."

"Most of Rose was absent, huh?"

"I know you can't remember it so well, but that is the truth. At the same time, many of them remember the event as it unfolded, despite not being present. They must've been informed heavily on the details, almost as if Rose was meant to be a scapegoat for the heads of the gang."

Kuril looked down. "Rose is still my enemy, no matter what."

"You should at least be aware of what happened to the Violet. I'm very sorry for your loss, Kuril."

"Thank you."

Ten stood up. "I ask that you help bring me back to life. My cloud resides within me beyond death, which is why I am able to haunt you."

"If I do so, you are no longer a Rose member. You will no longer cooperate with them."

"I will not cooperate further with you either. After all, any more information I could give would become a hindrance to you."

Kuril stood up. "What do I need to do?"

"I was originally going to keep this a secret, but you need to kill me."

"Any pain I inflict on you is inflicted on me as well."

"Drown me again."

Kuril sighed. "That's harder than it looks."

"You will take in the deepest breath possible and I will exhale as much as I can. It should make this process a lot easier," Ten replied, slicking back his green hair. "Do you understand?"

Kuril nodded. "Go ahead."

Kuril inhaled as Ten exhaled. With his chest puffed out, Kuril reshaped his arm to become water, where he began to suffocate Ten. Inhaling the water, Ten quickly began to struggle. Kuril, on the other hand, felt that same pain, but knew his lungs would make it through. Ten's lungs filled with water intentionally as Kuril hit the wall behind him in pain. Ten hit the ground, where Kuril kept the bubble of water over him to make sure he would drown. Kuril's eyesight began to fade, but he was not yet ready to pull the plug on the plan. A few more seconds passed, resulting in Kuril to eventually give in and release the bubble.

Immediately gasping for air, Kuril stared at the body below him. As Ten opened his eyes, he banged his hand against the wall. Kuril, who was still trying to catch his breath, could not feel it at all.

"Did you feel it?" Ten asked.

"No," Kuril replied, still trying to maintain his breathing.

"Thank you, Kuril. If you ever need anything, I'll probably be long gone."

Kuril's breathing relaxed as his heartbeat became more prominent in his own senses. "Then you're going to start a new life?"

"Yeah."

"Would you rejoin Rose if I gave you the chance?"

"Without a doubt."

Kuril swallowed once again. "You're a man of your word, huh?"

"Yeah."

Kuril chuckled. "You can go off and live a real life now, alright?"

"Thank you."

Ten walked out of the alleyway as Kuril finally caught his breath. About ten seconds after, he left the area too, but could not spot Ten within the bustling crowds. Looking into the sunset, Kuril continued to drag his feet against the Velindas streets.

On top of a small building was Mia, crouching down and watching Kuril move. From there, the moon illuminated her perfectly. Her eyes, similar to Kuril's aquatic blue, shined as the full moon that rested behind her glowed a white aura. With the intent to kill for the sake of the plan that William devised, as well as her lust to kill the final full-blooded Violet, she looked down on the blond man.

"Kuril!" she yelled as he passed the building.

His eyes widened as the voice echoed through his head. Slowly turning his head, he saw Mia looking down on him. His jaw slightly stretched open as he looked on in terror at the sight of her.

"Mia."

Mia leaped down from the building and pounced on Kuril. Her cat-like attacks were hard for Kuril to prevent, but right now it was hard for him to even process that she was still alive. The people around backed up and watched the fight ensue, not willing to step in.

"How are you alive?" Kuril asked, gripping onto Mia's arms as she tried to reach for him.

"I'm going to settle this."

Kicking Mia off of him and getting back, Kuril liquified his arm, ready to counter whatever she would throw at him.

"You've grown weak, Kuril. Weren't you one of the strongest in the Violet?"

"I have not grown weak, Mia."

Her hands glowed. "Then why did you spare Ten?"

"What does mercy have to do with strength?"

Mia charged at Kuril. "Mercy is an excuse to create peace, and peace is an excuse for the weaker animal to retreat!"

Kuril flung his arm at Mia, getting her wet as she rushed at him. Reforming behind her head in the air, the blond man attempted to land a kick on her head, yet was met with a hand on his leg and one pupil locking eye contact. Slamming Kuril into the ground and jumping on him, Mia began to burn his chest.

"I'm two steps ahead of you," Mia said, giving a condescending look to her prey.

Kuril screamed in pain as his chest burnt up. Liquifying in an attempt to escape, he reformed behind her going for a similar blow with his hand. As Mia tried to grab his wrist, Kuril's other hand knocked hers back as she took a fist to the face. Being knocked back, Kuril continued with a few more punches. Mia retaliated by getting low and grabbing his arm, burning his wrist.

"I don't feel it," Kuril said, kneeing Mia in the chin, causing her to fall back.

Mia regained her balance as she lunged at Kuril again. However, while she was being sent backwards, Kuril threw a drop of water on the ground. Mia realized what Kuril had done when he reformed right behind her and grabbed her hair.

"I'm not as weak as you think." Kuril slammed her into the ground. "Mercy is just another skill I learned. I move forward. I move past things. I don't even want to kill you anymore. You're Violet. I'm Violet. We have no reason to fight."

Mia looked up at Kuril. "We hate each other. What more of a reason do we—"

"I don't hate you." Mia took note of Kuril's expression. "I only hate myself."

Mia swiftly stood back up and took Kuril to the ground, who did not fight back. Punching his face repeatedly, she took her anger out on him. "Why the fuck would you hate yourself?" she asked, stopping her fist for him to answer.

"I caused your pain."

"Why would you go through all that emotional turmoil for me?"

"I don't."

Mia punched him again. "Then why do you go through it?"

"I don't know how to express my emotions. I don't know how internal turmoil works. All I know is hate."

"Then what the fuck am I to you? You fucking hate me! You always have!"

"You're a symbol of how much I hate myself."

Mia's hand started to glow again. "Fuck you and your self-pity."

"We have things we want to protect, right?"

Mia's hand stopped glowing.

Kuril's blue eyes faded in color. "Before Twelve passed, she told me she wanted to protect you. I promised her I would. I can't believe I almost broke that promise."

Mia dropped her arm. "Do you have things you want to protect now, Kuril?"

"Yeah."

"I see."

Mia's hand glowed again and she grabbed onto Kuril's shoulder. "Why the fuck should you get that chance to protect something?"

Kuril yelped in pain, but started to slowly hold it in. "There is no such thing as deserving for me, I just want to protect instead of hurt for once in my life."

She removed her hand as it stopped glowing. "I don't know how to feel."

"You have something you want to protect, Mia."

She looked down into Kuril's eyes. The expression to kill was gone. "Yeah."

"Let's focus on that."

Mia paused. "Yeah."

Standing up, she walked away from Kuril slightly to give him room. Getting up after her, Kuril brushed the debris off of him. He was a mess. With burn marks across his chest and right shoulder, Kuril didn't look like he was doing so well. His shirt was burnt through and his right arm was trembling.

"I'm sorry," Mia said.

"I'm sorry."

"Kuril," Mia continued, "I never want to see you again after today."

Kuril looked diagonal to him. He was staring at the ground with his head only slightly down. He smiled slightly with delicate eyes. It looked almost as if he wanted to cry, but he couldn't.

"We part ways here, Mia."

Mia turned toward one end of the street as Kuril directed his body to the other side. "I was supposed to kill you for a mission assigned by Three."

"What?"

"There is suspicion that One and Two want the rest of Rose dead for their own plan. We don't know what it is yet, but Twelve, Three, and I are trying to find out."

Kuril smiled. "Twelve is alive?"

"Yeah."

"I'm really happy to hear that."

Mia started to walk away. "Stay safe. We don't know what One and Two want with you."

"You only want me to be safe because you want Twelve to be safe."

Mia walked away without responding. Kuril started to walk in his direction as well, on his way back to the motel, oblivious to what had just occurred there. As he continued down the street, the people who were watching cleared the way for him. His shirt looked almost like a rag, his hair was messed up, and there was a slight amount of blood on him. His feet felt a little lighter now.

Kuril managed to return to the motel and saw Junil outside of the room, sipping a can of soda from the vending machine. There were a few police around the area as Kuril walked onto the property.

"You're a mess, Kuril." Junil looked him up and down. "What happened?"

"Nothing."

"No, seriously. What happened between you two?"

"We never fought."

Junil took a sip of his drink. "Then how did you end up looking like—"

"I already told you that nothing happened." Kuril looked at his motel room.

"Okay. I'm guessing no one died on your end."

"What went down here?" Kuril asked.

"There's a lot of blood in there, we might have to move to my place."

"Where are you staying?"

"I live on the top floor of the Velindas Hotel."

Kuril sighed. "The fancy detective has the top floor of a hotel."

Junil's face was blank. "The top five is all that remains, but Kaylin got hurt."

Catching the memo, Kuril went on to the next topic. "Is Kaylin going to be okay?"

"No doubt. She'll be fine."

"Want to go on a walk to your hotel room then?"

"Why not?" Junil took another sip and started walking.

Kuril sighed. "I need to get a new set of clothes first."

"Go ahead."

Kuril dodged the police, excusing himself each time he slid past an officer. Getting into his room, he grabbed a black tee and black jeans, which were very monotone, but at least slightly fashionable for him. Walking into his own bathroom, he noticed a police officer.

"Can I get changed?" he asked.

"What happened to you—"

"Get out of my bathroom."

The police officer rushed out of the bathroom. Kuril shut the door and changed into his new clothes, which complimented him a lot more than his old outfit. Stretching slightly, he flinched as the burn mark spiked in pain. Leaving the bathroom and tossing his old clothes onto a small pile in the corner of the motel room, Kuril yawned. He was pretty exhausted. Kuril walked out of the motel room, noticing the detective facing the city and away from Kuril.

"I'm ready," Kuril said.

"Then let's get going," Junil replied without looking back.

The two partners took their walk together across the business side of the city and into the hotel districts. This was the first time they walked together in a few days, but they've made remarkable progress since. The fight was nearing the end, but they knew the final five was not an easy lineup.

While the final five was strong, the final two, the heads of Rose, were even greater in strength. Adam and James were once in a lifetime. To Junil, he felt powerless. All he could do was strategize, but the fighting experience by the two heads of Rose would overpower all his ideas. Kuril didn't worry, he felt as if he had no time for that. Kuril only looked forward, not worrying about the deep water he was walking into.

Junil's trench coat flew back as the wind blew against the two of them. Kuril's plain white shirt usually was covered by a suit, but the fighting conditions in such a hot city didn't make it necessary.

"James visited Kaylin and I," Junil spoke.

"What?" Kuril looked over at Junil's face.

"He saved us. He shot both Eight and Six, two bullets each, all in the head."

"Why would he save the enemy?" Kuril asked.

"James was angered that they hurt Kaylin, so he took them out. Before we parted ways, he told me I was a good man."

"This doesn't make sense, that was his chance to end the war."

"I can't figure anything out, but maybe he wants us alive for a little longer."

Kuril and Junil kept walking, thinking about what Junil proposed as an answer.

"Why would he want us alive?" Kuril asked himself out loud.

Junil ran his hand through his hair, being blown by the occasional wind. "Maybe James wants Rose gone."

"That doesn't make sense," Kuril replied, "why would he do that when he can just disband Rose?"

"I have no idea."

"Adam told me something." Kuril looked ahead at the road.

"What did he say?"

"He said that you're his opponent."

"That makes sense," Junil replied, sighing immediately after.

Kuril looked over at Junil again. "He said the Rose members were just pawns."

"Something isn't right."

"A lot of things need to be cleared up."

"All we can do is fight and get justice."

"I suppose so," Kuril replied.

"We're almost at the hotel."

"It's that close?" Kuril asked.

"It's not very far away."

On James' walk back to his base of operations, he blended in with the people around him. Though his purple coat wasn't flashy, it wasn't the usual business attire you'd see on this side of the city. As he continued to walk, he saw a familiar face stand in his path.

It was a face he wanted to see so badly, but a face that he never wanted to see again.

"Abigail." James' eyes widened. "Is that you?"

"James, I want to talk."

"I thought I told you to leave me in the past."

"Please, just talk to me!" she pleaded.

"What do you want?"

"Can we settle this over dinner?"

James looked up at the sky as his method of telling time. Sure, it was late, but James didn't mind either way. "Sure, but don't expect anything."

She walked over to him and grabbed his hand. "I know a spot."

James embraced his hands in hers. "Let's go."

Abigail and James were childhood friends, or some would call practically lovers. James was so foreign to the concept of romantic love that nothing ever sparked between them, but it was obvious that if someone in their hometown of Norman got married, it would be one of them with the other. The two were so close as children, but barely kept in touch after the creation of Rose. Abigail knew James' secret, but didn't want it to ruin the love between them, even if it was dwindling every minute.

As the two made it into the restaurant, James took it up to ask about the sudden meeting. "Where did you find me?"

"I just went on a walk," Abigail said, "it was fate that I wanted to and that I did see you."

"Did you personally search for me?"

Abigail brushed her black bangs to the side a little. "Would it feed your ego if I said yes?"

"You can't feed something that doesn't exist."

"Wow, someone changed."

James chuckled. "Yeah, I did. You only got cuter."

"You're really something." Abigail laughed with James as they waited to be served.

"Reminds me of our nearly nonexistent teenage years."

The two were directed to their seats, where they were immediately given menus and provided with water in wine glasses. The restaurant was clearly fancy, and James had no idea if Abigail could afford it.

"What are you going to eat?" James asked.

"I don't know yet, we just got here."

"I'll just get a side order."

Abigail took her eyes away from the menu and toward James. "Is your stomach still weak?"

"It's getting harder to eat every day."

"Have you considered seeking medical help?"

"I don't believe that's necessary," James said, "I'm not going to be alive much longer. I also have no identity."

"Don't say that."

"How much longer can I go with a failing body?"

"Stop it, James."

James' eyes were neutral as they looked into Abigail's eyes. "I apologize."

The two sat in silence staring at the menus. James put his menu down a lot quicker than Abigail did, but didn't bother to look at her. He just looked down at the table. It was clear he wasn't feeling well. For a long time, James hasn't been feeling well.

After a few minutes of that silence, the waiters came to take their orders. Abigail got a full meal, but James only got a side order. James was suffering from a medical condition that made it hard to eat. Ever since James was a child, he was used to constantly eating less and puking more. It didn't stop him from forcing food into his body so he could grow, but that type of action only made his stomach worse.

"James," Abigail started, "is there another reason as to why you are going to die?"

"Someone's going to kill me."

"Is it that private detective?"

"I don't know who's going to kill me."

Abigail's voice grew more serious. "Look at me, James."

James looked at Abigail, and there he saw the person who helped him through everything. He saw the girl he loved for so long, but was unable to do anything. He couldn't ever break her by expressing that love. He didn't have it in him. The head of Rose saw the most beautiful woman on the inside and the outside, and she was right in front of him.

"You'll be okay as long as I'm here." Abigail's face brightened up, yet James could easily tell it was a mask she wore to hide the undeniable truth: she could never protect him, even if she wanted to try.

"Are you sure?" James asked.

"I'll be right here with you through everything."

"Will I be safe?"

"Of course you will."

James smiled and closed his eyes. "Thank you, Abigail."

Her voice took a pleading, yet grieving tone, which was contrary to her previous attitude. "Please, just let me help you."

James didn't feel like responding.

The two of them moved past the gloomy topics, and went on to talk about their past and how the present is treating them. Abigail and James had so many memories to reminisce on, but from the looks of it, both of them hadn't moved on from each other.

"You've taken on modeling?" James asked.

"It's a nice profession," she responded, "especially when it makes you popular."

"Well, it sounds like you aren't very popular with anyone besides me."

"Come on! I got my own fanbase!"

James chuckled. "I haven't seen them."

"I'm actually on a billboard by the hotel district!"

"Oh?"

Abigail turned her eyes away. "I wish."

"It's okay, you got the looks to go a long way."

"That means nothing coming from you."

"Is it because I'm so used to your beauty?" James joked.

"You flatter me."

The food arrived at their table. James only had a plate of potato wedges, while Abigail had a full pescetarian meal that James never even saw before. The place was lively for sure, and that was just based on how prepared the food was.

"Are you enjoying your food?" James asked.

"It's delicious." Abigail looked over at James. "Are you enjoying yours?"

James smiled and threw his head back. "Lord, I thank thee for the plate of potato wedges before me."

Abigail loved seeing that joker side of James. It was almost like he was slowly feeling better and gaining his will to live again. James went back to eating, but noticed her bright smile. It was beautiful, and it reminded James that in such a dark world, there was beauty.

Once the two finished their meal, they paid the check and took their leave. It was a good night for James, who had no regret spending it with Abigail. The model was more than happy to spend it with the head of Rose, who she was searching for this entire time.

James decided to walk Abigail back to her apartment to embrace the last moments of the day. As the two walked, James grabbed her hand. He felt whole again with her, and all his sins were washed away in her presence. He didn't need to worry about anything right now. Focusing on Abigail was all he could do.

On their walk, James felt weak. His body suddenly changed the entire mood. He let go of Abigail's hand and ran into an alleyway by the side, where he puked up everything he ate from the entire day. James' condition was only getting worse. He needed to see a doctor soon. It was never easy though, because he had no identity. James was nobody, and he hasn't been since he was a teenage boy.

His sides started to clench up as his muscles tightened up. Abigail chased after him into the alleyway.

James tried to catch his breath. "I'm so sorry—"

"Stop apologizing!" Abigail raised her voice.

James wiped the saliva that was dripping from his lips with his coat, then looked at Abigail. "I'm sorry."

"Did you not hear me?"

James didn't respond as he took his time to find his words.

"Are you okay? Can you walk?"

"I think I'll be able to make it to your place. It's just around the corner, right?"

Abigail grabbed James' hand this time. "Let's go."

The girl looked back at the alleyway, noticing that James' vomit was not just food, but also blood—a development she was not aware of. As she slowly paced away from the alleyway, locking palms with James, her mind questioned how much fuel he had left in him.

She directed him to her apartment, which was located on the northern side of the business part of Velindas. Entering the building, Abigail and James went into the elevator immediately, not stopping for anything.

In the elevator, James grabbed onto the railing to hold himself up. His vision started to give in as his body drained itself of energy. Abigail let go of his hand so he could support himself as the elevator moved.

"Stay here for the night," Abigail demanded. "I'm not letting you leave like this."

"Okay."

The elevator doors opened, and Abigail grabbed James' hand again. She directed him into her apartment, which was somewhat small, but able to fit two people without a doubt. She placed James on her bed, where he closed his eyes.

"Water, please," he begged.

Abigail went into the kitchen and ran the tap, putting some

water in a glass cup. She quickly hurried back to James and supported his body to sit up so he could drink the water before laying down again. After James drank the water, he fell back onto her mattress. To James, that mattress felt like heaven. His eyes had given up on him, and he closed them. James passed out. He was fatigued, stressed, running on no energy, and barely able to move.

"You're going to be okay," Abigail softly spoke, running her hands through his hair, "I'm going to make sure of that."

That night lasted forever for Abigail, and she spent every minute of it cherishing James. However, as long as it lasted, she fell asleep. James woke up and dragged himself out of the bed, ready to continue his business as usual.

CHAPTER VII

When Junil was twelve, Adam was about to turn thirteen. That's the way it always was. Junil's birthday was very close to Adam's birthday, but there was still a gap between them by one year and a week. As Adam's birthday was approaching, news broke out at the orphanage: Anna was sexually assaulted by the headmaster, Jacoby Brown.

"I don't get it at all," Junil said. "Who would do that?"

Adam sat across from him at a table, where the two ate their lunch alone. "The world is filled with bad people, Junil."

"Anna usually sits with us, but she's away now."

"I think we'll get back together soon. Maybe even before my birthday."

Junil slurped his soup. "It won't happen."

"Why not?" Adam looked up at Junil.

"I want justice," Junil responded, "even if I have to do it by force."

"I know you and Anna were close, but—"

"You can't change my mind."

Adam's spoon toyed with the food around it. He had no response. The rest of their lunch time was going to be spent in silence. Adam had no idea what Junil wanted to do, but Junil wanted to keep it that way.

"I don't recommend taking action, Junil. We could formulate a plan to make sure Mr. Brown is jailed. I know how strong your sense of justice is, but you need to be patient."

"I'm going to take action."

"Don't."

"Adam, please trust me."

"You're in a state of mind."

Junil looked away. "Let's drop this."

Adam paused. "Okay."

Around midnight when all the children were asleep, Junil rose from his bed. Only Adam was awake, who usually liked to stay up and read a book he stole from the orphanage's library. Adam and Junil's beds were by the entrance, yet right next to each other as well. This was convenient for Junil if he wanted to slip out in silence.

The door creaked a little as Junil tried to open it. Pausing to make sure no one woke up, Junil checked his surroundings. Adam was looking at him.

"Where are you going?" Adam asked.

"I'm only going to the bathroom."

Junil silently slipped himself through the crack of the door and didn't bother to close it behind him. Junil knew the headmaster's dorm was never locked. Why would it be locked? There's no good reason. The brown-haired child walked in the halls, his footsteps barely making noises as his socks went further along the carpet.

Junil walked into the empty cafeteria, where he went behind the kitchen counter. Remaining silent, he opened a few drawers and took the sharpest knife he could find.

Junil always had a strong sense of justice. He believed in the idea that what goes around must come around, but his anger fueled that justice. The future detective wasn't alone with such ideas, as Adam thought the exact same way. The only difference was that Adam wasn't fueled with hate, he was only fueled with the desire to make the world a better place. Adam's sense of justice was innocent and altruistic.

The cafeteria was silent, but the deadly aura radiating from Junil was loud. The half-Violet orphan wasn't scared to stain his hands with murder, but he never did. Junil grew up in a rough spot, which didn't allow empathy to grow. He had no remorse for anyone who did him wrong, solely because he never developed that sense. Junil's entire world was just him, Adam, and Anna.

He trotted out of the cafeteria, knife in hand. Junil walked his final flight of stairs of freedom. On the second floor, he found the headmaster's office, which was also a bedroom in the back. Slightly opening the door, he found the headmaster asleep.

Junil wasn't going to let anything come in between the two of them. This orphanage was going to be stained with blood. The children would be scarred as their favorite headmaster ends up stabbed to death. To the kid who was in the headmaster's office, it didn't matter.

He walked toward the bed silently, where the headmaster was asleep. Raising the knife, Junil hesitated. He didn't know how to feel. It wasn't about taking someone's life, but it was about the fact that everything he had built in his life was going to be destroyed again, just like when his mother died and he was sent to an orphanage as a stranger to the children there. He came to this orphanage with nothing, but it struck Junil that he was also going to be leaving it with nothing.

The thought left his mind. The knife was plunged into the headmaster's heart, to where he woke up. Unable to react properly, Junil removed the knife and continually stabbed the same area. In a panic that the headmaster wasn't dying, he started to jab the knife in the stomach and soon forcefully dug it further into his chest. During that period of time, the headmaster let out a small sound, which wouldn't let Junil know if someone was alerted or not.

"I didn't think it would come to this," a familiar voice at the door spoke.

In an instant, Junil was on the ground, the blood over him, but the knife was out of his hands. Adam was in front of him, holding the knife. He had stopped time in order to set up a perfect scene: one in which Junil looked like a victim, but Adam was the guilty one.

"Junil, I'm going to have to punish you."

"Adam?"

"Let me stab you in the side to make you look like a victim."

"Adam, stop."

Adam slashed Junil's side with the knife. Junil remained on the floor and yelped in pain.

"Why, Adam!?"

"Stay there. From here on out, I killed Mr. Brown."

Junil's eyes widened. "You can't be serious, Adam."

"Please, just let me repay you."

"I didn't do anything."

Adam smiled at Junil. "You're going to be the world's best detective when we reunite. I know it."

"I'll never be a detective like my mother was. The job is stained by the police force—"

"Work privately, get stuff done privately. You'll be the greatest detective in the whole world."

"Adam, please just put down the knife and leave."

"I can't."

A crowd of footsteps ran into the room after hearing Junil's cry. There they saw Adam with a knife. The workers crowded the door as the children blissfully slept amidst the chaos. The handful of people stared in shock at Adam.

"Why would you do this?" one of them asked.

"Isn't it beautiful? The art of death? How when we die we just move on into some crazy world we call heaven? Wouldn't Mr. Brown want to experience that?"

Junil knew Adam was acting insane just to create a case for all of this. He wanted to speak up, but he found out why Adam sacrificed himself: no one knew Adam had a cloud, but everyone knew Junil did.

If it was determined that Junil was the killer, he would be killed himself. Adam would only receive legal punishment, psychiatry, and all the stuff that came along with it. Junil couldn't speak up. Junil still felt the pain in his side, but the pain that he was going to lose one of the few people he loved again hurt even more.

Someone had already contacted the police. Screams were going around, children were being woken up, and the deadly intent Junil once held was gone. There was nothing in Junil.

The police eventually arrived, but the scene never changed. No one dared to enter the room with Adam, Junil, and Mr. Brown's corpse before the police arrived.

As the police ran into the room, Adam dropped the knife and put his hands up. Adam was apprehended as Junil was comforted by the police. Adam and Junil were guided out of the room. The two split for a long time, not to meet again until they became adults.

Junil remained in the orphanage for a long time. Anna never returned. Adam was never going to come back. At lunch time, he was no longer alone. People comforted him all the time. He lost his friend, but became popular for being a tool of expressing sympathy. Time would go on and all Junil could do was embrace the dirty comments about Adam. Junil wanted justice for his own friend, but he was too scared to admit he was the killer. Junil would eventually leave that orphanage and join a wealthy family, where his detective skills would be sharpened.

Arriving at the entrance, Junil and Kuril were greeted by a fancy hotel, encompassed by gold-like walls, though the two of them knew it was just normal material. Bright lights way above their heads illuminated the peaceful hotel. People were doing a mixture of things from reading the newspaper to throwing pennies in the lobby's fountain.

"Have you ever been in an elevator?" Junil asked.

"Do you take me for some kind of caveman?" Kuril sighed and walked into the elevator alongside Junil.

Junil pressed the button with the fiftieth floor and put his back to the elevator wall.

"Do you need to get back to the motel for some stuff?"

"Just leave it behind, nothing was important."

"Clothes?"

"I'll use yours, we're probably the same size."

"Alright."

The elevator reached the fiftieth floor, where there was a short hallway ahead. The hallway led to three different doors.

"My room is the one on the left," Junil said.

Junil directed Kuril to his room. Inputting a code into a panel next to the door, Junil opened the hotel room. Inside that hotel room was a luxurious palace. The two walls on the outside were fully windows, allowing the two to see the city from fifty stories up.

"This is a really nice place, Junil."

"I get it free."

"No need to brag."

The two sat down and relaxed.

"Really? Only two beds again?" Kuril sighed. "I really don't like taking the floor."

"There's a couch."

"Oh, you can sleep on those?" Kuril shifted his head.

"You're a caveman."

Junil's phone rang, Adam was calling. Junil was starting to grow exhausted from these calls.

"Here we go again," Junil said.

Junil picked up the call, only to hear a voice he heard not too long ago.

"This is James."

"James?" Junil looked over at Kuril.

Junil put his phone on speaker so Kuril could listen in on the call.

"By any chance, could I meet with Kuril?" James asked.

Junil and Kuril looked at each other. Their eyes were widened, both just trying to read each other's fear to see if they were on the same page.

"As a fight?" Junil responded with a question.

"Only a meeting."

"Who else is showing up?"

"Just the two of us," James answered.

Junil looked at Kuril. Kuril nodded, giving the signal that he was willing to meet James.

"I accept on one condition."

"And that is?"

"I want to face Five. Before your meeting, tell Five to meet me on the roof of the Velindas Hotel. I know she can get there very easily. Tell her I'll lock the hotel down just for the fight."

"You sound like you have a personal grudge, Mr. Junil."

"I do."

"I'll notify Five to meet you at the Velindas Hotel rooftop. Both the meeting and the fight will be scheduled for midnight. I apologize if that intrudes on your sleep schedule."

"Where are you and Kuril meeting?"

"The empty lot by Zipline. Please call my actual phone when you complete your fight."

"What's the number?"

Junil and James exchanged numbers, something the both of them didn't think would happen when this war started.

"I'll contact you when my fight is finished," Junil said. "Thanks."

James hung up from Adam's phone. Junil and Kuril sat in the hotel room thinking. It was about five hours until midnight. Kaylin was going to be in medical care the entire night. Kuril started to lay down on the couch.

"I could use a fucking massage," Kuril said, taking off his shirt.

"I'm not giving you a massage."

"I know, but this couch is so soft I need to feel it with my own skin."

"Don't strip down."

Kuril sighed. "I didn't plan on it."

Junil grabbed his phone and contacted someone. The phone rang for a few seconds, and then someone picked up.

"Yanni, tell the department that they need to issue an evacuation for everyone in the Velindas Hotel. There's a Rose member in here with an explosive cloud. I've held them down for some time, but they may act. Inform the department that no personnel can enter the building, this is my mission."

Junil hung up.

"What was that about?" Kuril asked.

"Sometimes you have to lie."

"What was the call?"

"I needed to get the hotel in lockdown for a perfect battlefield against Anna."

"So everyone is going to be evacuated?"

"Very soon."

"How is Anna going to get in?"

"She's already here," Junil confirmed.

"How do you know?"

"Adam has a lot of intel."

"I'd imagine."

Kuril stood up and went toward the door. "I'm going to head out before the evacuation starts."

Kuril left the room. Junil stood up and followed him.

"Are you able to take the elevator alone?" Junil jested.

"I can."

"Then good luck."

"As with you."

Without further words being spoken, Junil went to the stairs instead of the elevator, marking the separating point of Kuril and Junil. Taking the stairs to the roof, Junil reached the windy rooftop. He sat down against the wall and waited calmly for Anna to arrive. Evacuations started.

People outside were making noise as the hotel was being emptied. Junil stayed out of sight on top of the roof. Opening the roof door were two people: a man with long black hair that was slicked back and a girl with brown, curly hair. With a finger gun to her throat, the man walked onto the rooftop and noticed Junil.

"Don't move or I'll use my cloud and kill her."

"I don't care," Junil replied.

"What?"

"You're both Rose members, aren't you?"

"How would you know?"

"Five and Four. I didn't think Five would so cheaply bring Four into the game."

"I'm holding her hostage!" yelled Four.

"Then I'll save her."

"Sit still."

Four pointed the finger gun at Junil, ready to fire. Junil, not knowing how fast it was, tried to predict the movement of the laser by immediately moving out of the way. This form of bait was met with a reaction by Four, making him fire accidentally. Junil confirmed that the laser was deadly, moving extremely fast. In fact, it was too fast for anyone to try and dodge.

There was one thing Kaylin was wrong about though: the laser bullet didn't destroy everything in its path. The bullet would do significant damage to just about anything and would easily kill a human. It could even kill a whole line of humans.

"Why the hell are you trying to kill me? I want to help you!" Junil yelled.

"Help me?" Four asked, aiming at Junil.

"You don't understand what's going on?" Junil's eyes were focused on the finger gun being pointed at him. He'd have to make a good prediction or his life would end.

"Enlighten me," replied Four.

Junil only said those lines to stall and try to find a way back into the hotel so he could use the closed area to his advantage.

Four whispered into Anna's ear.

"I refuse," she responded.

Junil had no idea what was going on, but tried to act like he heard it.

Junil inched himself toward the door. "Why would you refuse? It's your grand opportunity."

"So you know the truth?" Four asked.

"Of course."

"Admitting it was an awful idea," Four said, adjusting his aim to Junil.

Wind blew across the hotel roof. Junil's long brown hair flew as his trench coat did. As the gust of wind stopped, he realized he had no plan.

"Can I talk with Five in private?" Junil asked, putting his hands up.

"She's a hostage."

"Both of you are Rose members," Junil pointed out, "you don't need to hide it."

As another gust of wind blew past them, Four loosened his position on Junil and lowered the gun.

"Are you okay with this, Five?" Four asked.

"Sure."

Junil's escape was just an idea off the top of his head. Anna walked toward Junil, her small, yet strong figure getting closer as the wind blew harder. Anna was short, her height being only two inches above Junil's shoulders.

Junil smiled. "It's been a while, my love."

"I missed you, Junil." Anna plunged her head into Junil's shoulder and wrapped her arms around him. "You have no idea how much I missed you."

"I missed you too." Junil accepted the hug.

"I'm confused." Four tilted his head. "Do you two know each other?"

"We used to be a thing." Junil's face glowed, still holding Anna in his arms.

"That's why you didn't want to fight him, Five?" Four asked.

"I couldn't fight him, he's the only man I ever loved." Anna was still embracing Junil, but her voice was loud enough to be heard across the hotel roof.

Junil put his head across from Anna's temple to move in. While it looked like a lover's embrace to Four, it really wasn't.

"Anna, who are you sided with?" Junil whispered, barely opening his mouth.

Anna knew she had to whisper. "I'm with you."

"Then help me eliminate Four."

Anna went silent. She sniffed Junil's hair, which smelled of mint shampoo and sweat. She wanted to embrace Junil for a little longer before giving her answer, but she knew how impatient Junil was.

"I'll help you," she replied, "but after this..."

She didn't finish her sentence.

"What was that?" Junil whispered back.

"Let's run away."

"After we eliminate Four, I'll go anywhere with you."

"Okay."

The hug ended abruptly. Anna backed up, almost as if she were prey and Junil was a predator.

"How could you say that?" Anna's face grew pale.

Junil had no idea what was going on at the moment.

"You're a monster." Anna ran back to Four.

"Do I have permission to kill?" Four asked.

Anna faced Four and got in front of his line of sight. She stretched her arms and legs out to show that Four didn't have permission to fire.

"What is it now?" Four groaned.

"Junil has a reflective cloud. He will find a way to reflect your own laser at you."

Junil, listening in, started to grasp what was happening. Anna was lying for his sake. He had no idea if she had a plan or not.

"So how do I kill him?" Four asked.

"I've tied a piece of invisible string to him and I can attach the other end to you. I'll shorten the length and he'll have no time to reflect if you're close."

"Go ahead and fix me up then." Four kept a close eye on Junil. "You can stay there."

Anna got on one knee and started to tie a piece of string to Four's ankle.

"What's going on?" Junil asked.

Four smiled. "Send a prayer to God."

"What do you mean?"

"I'm done," Anna said, looking up to Four.

Standing up, Anna revealed the visibility of the string. The string was tied to Four's ankle and attached to Anna's finger.

"I thought you said the other part of the string was attached to him?" Four's eyebrow raised at Anna.

"I'm sorry."

The string tightened up and Anna flung her arm, launching Four in the air. Immediately, she whipped her arm like a sidearm baseball pitcher and sent Four off the roof. The string disintegrated and Four was already launched off the roof. He had no words. Four was not a man for last words, but rather, last actions. He aimed at Anna and shot a laser, but she moved out of the line of fire.

Falling onto the ground in her attempt to dodge, Anna stayed on her knees as Junil walked toward her. Anna never liked to kill people. Her hands weren't clean, but weren't as dirty as the rest of the Rose members.

Junil stood in front of Anna as she stayed on the roof.

Junil sighed. "It was hard, wasn't it?"

"I hate killing people."

"I can see that."

There was silence following the small talk as she stayed on the floor.

The Velindas-based detective ended the silence. "Let's go inside."

Junil reached his hand out to Anna. Grabbing it, her warm hands met Junil's cold hands. The heat mixed around and quickly turned Junil's hand warm. The two of them held hands as they walked into the hotel.

"How long has it been?" Anna asked.

"Too long for me."

"Are you and Adam still in touch?"

"Of course."

"Nothing really comes between you two."

Junil didn't respond.

Exiting the emergency staircase, Anna and Junil walked on the top floor hallway, which only had the elevator, staircase, and three doors leading to three individual suites.

"Where will we run to?" Anna looked at Junil's face.

"I'm not going anywhere with you."

"What?"

"Why did you lie about Mr. Brown sexually assaulting you?"

Anna took her time to find her words. "I wanted to leave the orphanage somehow. I was feeling trapped."

"You took Adam away from me."

"I didn't know that was going to happen."

"Adam told me it was a lie."

Anna smiled. "You guys are still friends, right?"

Junil let go of Anna's hand and immediately punched her across the face. Falling to the floor, Junil grabbed her by the hair with his left hand. His left hand glowed orange, rendering Anna useless. Still holding her by the hair, Junil kneed her face several times. In his swift movements, he threw her to the ground and started to repeatedly punch her in the face.

Junil never intended on going anywhere with Anna. Ever since that specific incident, he's been focused on one thing: revenge for Adam. The hatred that fueled him as a detective had to be lashed out in the form of physical violence.

"Are you kidding me?" Junil yelled.

Anna could move again. She gained space between the two of them, knowing that Junil had a small range for his cloud. Barely able to move, Anna pressed the elevator door button as a route for escape.

"So you were going to ruin Mr. Brown's life?!" Junil continued to rant. "You wanted to leave a fucking orphanage and ended up ruining the lives of three people?!"

Junil approached Anna slowly, knowing he could instantly kill her. Anna shot string out in a way to restrain Junil, but she realized the worst: the hallway had nothing for the string to latch onto. She sent the string to tie Junil's right hand and left leg together. Junil waited a few seconds for the cooldown of his cloud and then placed his left hand on the string that restrained two of his limbs. The string disintegrated easily.

Junil's cloud, the ability to power up or lessen the power of something, was perfect against Anna's cloud. His left hand could easily just get rid of any of the string.

"Leave me alone!" Anna screamed.

The elevator door opened as she scurried in. Her body was in sharp pain as she barely managed through the elevator doors. Junil came for the elevator like a ticking time bomb that would end Anna's life. Anna pressed a random floor and the button for the door to close. As the door almost closed, Anna gave a sigh of relief. The elevator door opened again as Junil's foot stood between the two sliding doors. Opening back up, Anna saw the full deadly intent of the man in front of her.

Junil walked into the elevator. "This is your death bed."

Junil's stare pierced Anna's eyes. He was intent on ending her life from the minute he found out the truth that Anna lied about Mr. Brown's sexual assault case. Her selfish desires got in the way of Junil's friendship with Adam. In fact, her own desires ruined Adam's life. Junil wanted nothing except pain on Anna.

"It's more complicated than that, Junil!"

Junil grabbed her head and slammed it into the back of the elevator several times. Anna was losing her sight. Junil grabbed a switchblade out of his pocket.

"This is where you suffer the same fate as Mr. Brown," Junil said.

"No…"

Shooting a string right at Junil's eyes, Junil was immediately blinded by the fibers that blocked his vision. With Junil unable to see, Anna kicked him across the elevator as he held onto his face.

"You fucking bitch!"

Anna brought herself to stand up straight. "Fibers, unlock."

The string sent at Junil's eyes disintegrated, causing a burning sensation in his eyeballs.

"Your cornea is facing apoptosis at such rapid levels that cells cannot build as quickly as they're dying." Anna collected herself, knowing that she held the upper hand. "In other words, your eyes are burning because your cells are killing themselves. That is the true power of my string."

"I don't need two eyes to kill you!"

"If you even think I am the person to worry about"—Anna kept distance between her and Junil, who was clenching his knife and covering his eyes in pain—"I never killed Four. He landed safely on a web of fibers I made."

"So you're saying…"

"All the police lined up outside of the building are going to fall victim to Four."

Junil's left hand glowed orange as he covered his eyes. He moved his hands away from his eyes as they remained closed. "I negated the cellular destruction."

"It'll return after your cooldown, no?"

"Not if you're dead."

Anna chuckled. "You're always the star of the show. Maybe that's why I loved you."

Junil slashed at where he heard the voice come from. The elevator, being small, didn't give Anna much space to dodge the switchblade. Getting slashed in her side, Anna fell even further back. Hearing the thud of Anna falling back, Junil charged again, hoping to hit the same side. Junil's slash followed through and Anna's panic couldn't save her.

Junil's right hand reached for the cut. Quickly observing the area and finding the blood, his hand glowed blue on the slash. Immediately restraining that hand to the railing in the elevator, Junil could no longer use his right hand. She screamed as she realized what Junil had done to her.

"If you're going to kill the cells in my eyes, I'm going to make your broken blood vessels overactive." Junil, being restrained to the corner of the elevator, wasn't able to make another move. "This is a pretty destructive fight."

Anna tried getting up off the elevator she fell onto during the panic, but she immediately fell back down. Both parties were unable to move. It was almost as if it were a waiting game.

"You know, those damaged cells are also going through apoptosis. It's the natural part of the cell cycle."

Anna stayed silent.

"How much blood is gushing out, Anna?"

She refused to speak. Her mind was trying to plan something.

"My little cooldown is up. Unfortunately, the energy I added to your damaged blood vessels isn't going to fade away immediately."

Anna used her string to create a bandage-like patch for her side. "It was a clever plan, but it won't work on me."

Junil announced his deduction, "You can't use your weird apoptosis ability again, huh?"

"You're right."

Anna sent a string right at Junil's head. "I can kill you right here. Do you have any last words?"

"Checkmate."

Junil's free hand touched the string and all of the fibers disappeared, including the patch Anna had. The blood that built up inside of her gushed out onto the elevator floor and onto her body.

"Touching any of your strings with my negative hand nullifies all your strings," Junil explained, regaining his composure. "It was only natural that I couldn't reach the string that restrained my other hand."

Anna's face grew pale as she yelled in agony and fell to the floor.

Junil continued, "I wish I could see what your face looks like right now."

Anna looked up at Junil's smile, which gave an eerie aura to her, even with his eyes shut. Her mouth let out a few noises as it barely hung open.

"Goodbye, Anna."

The switchblade went straight into Anna's heart. It was as simple as that. The years built up at the orphanage meant nothing to Junil. The detective didn't care anymore. The pain he felt when Adam took the blame for him was enough to make him angry at himself, but when he found out Anna lied, he immediately put it on her. All that anger and hatred that built up was directed toward Anna.

The elevator doors remained shut as Junil pressed the lobby button. Anna's dead body laid on the ground. Junil took a seat next to her and looked at the elevator roof. He found himself in the same shoes from when he was twelve. The only difference this time is that he enjoyed it. The Phantom of Velindas enjoyed taking the life of his childhood love. He was satisfied beyond words to get his revenge.

Junil looked up at the security camera, which watched the entire thing. Though no one was in the building at the time, Junil's eyelids were facing directly toward the camera. He smirked as his closed eyes faced directly at the camera lens.

Junil chuckled. "Four remain, huh?"

The doors opened to the lobby. At that point, Junil had already passed out next to the corpse of Anna.

"Good morning, gentlemen!" Four walked behind the police forces that gathered around the giant hotel's parking lot.

"Who are you?" asked a senior officer.

"I'm Four." Four immediately shot a laser right through the senior officer's head.

Lucky for Four, he was surrounded by very few officers. No one saw what he had done except for a few onlooking officers. They aimed their guns at Four, but before they knew it, they were all shot dead too. The parking garage wasn't a very noticeable spot for murder.

Four stripped down and put on one of the police officer's uniforms, where he disguised himself in the crowd. After getting dressed, he walked toward the other side of the hotel, where the crowd of police was much larger. It was very easy for him to infiltrate from there, considering the police were too focused on the task at hand.

Four had noticed that the police were almost lined up horizontally, which would allow a laser to blast through most of their chests. Setting himself up at the end of the police, Four made a circle with one hand by touching his thumb and index finger and a finger gun with the other hand.

Four was limited to his lasers as if it were his own energy. He couldn't just shoot forever. However, he also possessed the ability to shoot through shapes he could make with his other hand. By shooting through those shapes, the laser would reshape itself to the shape of the hole. By creating a circle with his index finger and thumb and shooting through it, Four would just have a normal laser, but much larger—a bullet the size of the hole.

Four aligned his hands to aim and take fire. "I suppose this will be fun."

Officers fell to the ground as holes in their torsos and stomachs were made. Some even lost parts of their neck. Almost all of these officers were shot, and almost all of them were dead.

"Bang!" Four laughed.

Chaos ensued as the police scrambled to get to safety. From behind Four, a shot rang through the crowd. Four was shot in his arm. Turning around and clenching his teeth, he realized he was standing before the cousin of the Phantom of Velindas. The young detective's brown hair flew in the wind. He wore an industrial black coat over a white tee with black jeans, not very fitting for the weather in Velindas.

Yanni looked at Four directly in his eyes. "It's been windy recently."

Four aimed at Yanni. "Big fucking mistake."

"That's a little unfair for a shootout."

"Shut up."

The aura around Yanni was almost unsettling for the people around him. It was strong, radiating with potential. The detective had seen many things in his life, but never had he seen so many police officers die at once like that. His face was one filled with gloom and acceptance, as he looked down a little with a slight curve on his lips upward. He was grinning a little bit as he accepted the despair around him.

"I suppose that's life, huh?" Yanni said, breaking the ice.

"As in?"

The detective looked back up at Four. There was, in fact, a smile on his face. "People die in an instant. That's the nature of your cloud. It's so similar to a gun, but it leaves not a single moment for that person to think about themselves or their life."

"Life takes the people we love from us in an instant too. You can laugh and cheer with your friends and family, but will they be there tomorrow?" responded Four.

"Something terrible must have happened to you if you have a cloud with such meaning, huh?"

"I don't think much of it."

Yanni's face grew more grim. It was not his facial expression changing, but rather, the aura around him being enhanced by his words. "Are you growing impatient with that bullet in your arm?"

"I am, but you intrigue me."

Yanni tilted his head a little bit and chuckled, revealing his lackadaisical attitude. "Can I ask a question?"

"Go ahead."

"When you first achieved your cloud, did you understand it very well?"

Four took a second to think about his answer. "Yeah, I actually did understand my cloud immediately."

"Then that must be what this feeling is."

Four's eyes widened as Yanni continued to stare him down. "What do you mean?"

Yanni watched as Four's arm shook. "Is the poison kicking in so early?"

"What?"

Yanni took a lollipop out of his pocket. "I don't like to smoke, but this does the job." Taking off the wrapper and putting it in his mouth, Yanni grinned at the Rose member. "You'll die soon from that bullet."

"Why the hell would you lace a bullet with poison? That hasn't been legal in years—"

"It's not a big-shot poison. My cloud can lace anything with poison as long as I touch it. That bullet was laced from the very start." Yanni took the lollipop out of his mouth. "It's aconitine poison. It doesn't spread fast."

Police officers watched as Yanni confronted Four. They were astonished by his bravery and careless attitude. Four's eyes widened as his eyebrows slanted downward toward each other. He aimed his finger at his own arm where the bullet was fired and shot around the area. Police officers attempted to dodge the lasers that passed through him. Four screamed in agony as he made a hole in himself. Blood spewed out of his arm, pouring all over himself and the floor.

"Your turn." Four's shaking, unharmed arm aimed at the police officer.

Yanni put the lollipop back in his mouth. "I find it really unimaginable that you'd believe anything I said."

"What?"

"I lied to you. I suppose cognitive dissonance really got to you. That's the term, right? My real cloud is the ability for me to make anything you genuinely believe, such as a lie, real to only you for an hour at a time."

Four yelled, "You bastard!"

Jumping out of the way before Four could fire, Yanni barely escaped Four's laser. "I didn't exactly lie too much. Since you believed me, there really was poison inside of you."

Four fell to his knees as blood continuously leaked out of his body.

Yanni stood up and looked back at Four. "It really is strange how people can die in an instant."

Yanni turned back around as Four finally collapsed. The officer walked away from the body, declaring his victory. Yanni didn't know where he was walking. He just wanted to take his champion's stride. Turning his head one more time, Yanni finally put a bullet in Four's head to kill him.

The police got up and gathered around Yanni and Four. Many of them removed their caps for the fallen officers who died from the laser shot by Four. Yanni never wore a police cap, so he bowed his head to respect the ones who died.

"Come on, we have to check up on detective Junil," Yanni said, taking charge. "I'll get to him with the second squad. Everyone else needs to check on the current officers."

Yanni felt proud of what he did. To be fair, he only carried around that lollipop because he wanted to do something as carelessly heroic and calm as his cousin.

Kuril walked past Zipline and into an alleyway. The alleyway led to an empty lot, where James was waiting. Kuril was already prepared to come face-to-face with the man who directed the charge against the Violet, but he had no intention of getting violent at the time. Kuril walked into the empty lot, greeted by a man who was about an inch taller than him.

"Are you Kuril?" the man asked.

"I am."

He smiled. "I'm James, the brother of Kaylin."

"You're also the leader of Rose."

James looked Kuril in the eyes. "Look to your left."

Looking to his left, Kuril saw Kaylin, who he believed to be in the hospital. She was closer to James than Kuril. Despite wearing her usual outfit of a long black skirt and sweater, her hair was a little more messy than wavy.

"Discharged in one day?" Kuril asked, surprised.

"The doctors said I was fine." Kaylin's fingers got fidgety.

James tossed a gun at Kuril. Unable to react swiftly, Kuril cupped the gun in his arms.

"Why are you giving me a gun?" the Violet asked.

James took out a knife and cut a line into his palm. Kaylin yelped in pain, but James was silent. He didn't feel like talking.

"Kaylin, put your hand out," James commanded.

Kaylin put her hand out exactly as James ordered. James put his hand out too. On both of their hands were slashes, but James only slashed his hand.

"What is this?" Kuril asked.

"This is my cloud's true ability. Kaylin never knew about this either." James' eyes were cold and dead. There was no life in them. "I lied about my cloud to her." James' stare went through Kuril's body.

"Why are you telling me?"

"I'm linked to Kaylin. There is no way you can remove this link between us."

"James, what's going on?" Kaylin asked.

James ignored Kaylin. "If you shoot Kaylin, I will die. If you shoot me, Kaylin will die. Either way, shoot one of us and we both die."

Kuril stared back at James.

"Are you going to end this fight? Are you going to avenge the Violet?" James asked.

"No."

"Why not?"

"I'm not hurting Kaylin."

"If you shoot one of us, the war ends. I'll be dead."

Kuril dropped the gun. "I'm not hurting Kaylin."

"Do you have some kind of attachment to my sister?"

Kuril wasn't scared to respond. "She's like a sister to me, just as she is to you. I want to protect her."

"So your decision is final?"

"I'm not hurting Kaylin."

Kuril's eyes opened. It was all a dream. He was awake in the empty lot, but James was still there. In fact, Kuril slept standing up. Kaylin was never there, she was still in the hospital.

James took it in him to start the conversation. "That's my true cloud. I can't send you to another world and I can't replicate pain or death onto someone else. My cloud is simple: I can make people dream by just looking into their eyes."

"So what I was told and what I just saw was a lie," Kuril

replied. "In fact, your real cloud is ocular and revolves around illusions. Am I correct?"

"You are."

"I understand," Kuril said, "you were testing me."

"I have your gratitude, Kuril. If you did hurt my sister, I wouldn't be so kind to you."

"You trust me with Kaylin?"

"I do."

"Can I ask something about your ability?"

"Go ahead," James replied.

"Can you make Kaylin see things?"

James' face dropped. "I can't."

"She'll never be able to see," Kuril responded.

James smiled. "She'll be able to see a new world when the Blooming Day happens."

The two exchanged words through their eyes. Kuril wanted to pursue answers regarding the Blooming Day, but he felt it would be useless. James, on the other hand, wanted to continue the discussion. Four eyes, each one speaking a million words, but only moving and staring.

"Is that it?" Kuril asked, ready to leave.

"You're a good person, Kuril."

"I still don't like you."

"I know."

"I'm still going to kill you."

James went silent and smiled.

"Are you going to kill the rest of the Rose members?" James asked.

"Why?"

"I'm curious."

"Do you want them dead or something?"

James chuckled at the line of questioning. "They're meaningless to me."

"That's harsh to your comrades."

"Don't you think the same of Junil?"

Kuril scoffed. "Junil is my teammate, but more importantly, he is my brother, no matter his affiliation with the Violet bloodline."

"You two have gotten close. Adam must be pretty jealous."

Kuril rolled his eyes. "That guy is a drag."

James laughed. "He can be a little too much sometimes."

Kuril didn't enjoy the small talk. "Is that all?"

"I must express my gratitude," James bowed down and offered his hand out as offering friendliness before the storm.

"No thanks," Kuril said.

"Shall you be going now?"

"Is there anything else?"

"No."

"Then I'll be leaving," the Violet spoke, walking away.

"Junil never contacted me, but it should be fine to go back to the hotel."

"Thanks."

"May I also have your contact information? I'd like our final encounter to be formal."

Kuril turned around. "You're really one for manners."

"Just how I was raised."

"For a savage, you aren't really a savage."

James chuckled. "Tomorrow marks the Blooming Day, you know. Or is it today now?"

"I'm going to guess you won't tell me any of the details."

James gave the Violet a smile. "Do not worry about tomorrow, for tomorrow will worry about itself. Each day has enough trouble of its own."

"Then we're done here."

Kuril walked out of the alleyway and into the street. As he made his way to the hotel, a few thoughts crossed his head. He wanted to know what the Blooming Day was, what the illusion was about, and why he even invited him.

Velindas was having a normal night. Everyone's morale was

up knowing that Rose members were dropping like flies, but no one understood what was really going on: Rose had plans that would shake the entire city. Rose could lose all their petals, but still find a way to bloom. That was the purpose of the Blooming Day.

CHAPTER VIII

Laying in the hospital bed with his eyes shut and hands folded, Junil patiently waited for assistance from the doctor. His door opened as the doctor walked in and took a seat next to the hospital bed.

"Well, it seems as if your eyes will be okay under one circumstance."

"What is it, doc?" Junil asked.

"You'll have to wear sunglasses."

"Forever?"

"Yes."

Junil groaned. "Do they look cool at least?"

"It's a reddish lens. I think it looks futuristic and stylish."

"How do they work?"

The doctor looked at his clipboard. "You will have to wear them whenever you want to open your eyes due to the cornea being permanently damaged. You don't have to wear them at night while you sleep."

"Are they ready for me, Dr. Shukar?"

"I brought your pair. It's being covered by the city of Velindas, so you don't have to pay anything for it."

Junil put on the sunglasses and jumped out of the bed. He swiftly walked over to the mirror in the hospital bed and observed how he looked in the mirror.

"Holy shit."

"What is it, Junil?" Dr. Shukar asked.

"I look awesome."

"I'm glad you like them."

"Oh, by the way"—Junil looked over at the doctor— "can I see someone?"

"A patient?"

"Yeah. Her name is Kaylin."

"I am her doctor, but I am not allowed to do that."

"I see. Is she doing well?"

The doctor looked back at his clipboard. "She's doing good. She's planned for discharge very soon."

"Glad to hear. I'll pick her up later. I know she's excited to see me."

Junil walked toward the door and waved at the doctor who waved back. Junil and the doctor had met many times before, so this was starting to become a common occurrence for them. Junil walked out of the hospital casually with his new sunglasses on.

Ignoring the crime scenes of Five and Four, Junil made it back to his hotel room pretty quickly. He yawned as he opened his door, barely taking note of Kuril. Jumping onto his bed, Junil groaned in exhaustion.

"Sounds like someone is finally back," the Violet spoke, watching the news.

"Sounds like someone didn't bother to check in on me."

"I knew you were okay."

"Even though there were two messy crime scenes?"

Kuril sighed. "Are you implying I overestimate you?"

"Did you even notice my new look?"

Kuril turned away from the television and looked at Junil. "Nice sunglasses."

"Two words?"

"Very nice sunglasses."

"You suck, Kuril."

Kuril looked back at the television. "Thanks."

Junil picked himself up on the bed and looked at the news. "Who's the cop who took down Four?"

"Yanni. He called me right after the mess and told me all about how cool he was."

"My cousin?"

"Yeah. It's all over the internet."

Junil's smile went cheek to cheek. "That's my boy, Yanni!"

The duo's peace was disturbed by a knock on the hotel room. Junil groaned yet again and looked over at the door as if it were miles away. The lazy detective eventually got up and walked toward the door, barely carrying himself across the room.

Opening the door, he saw a male about two inches shorter than him with his hands being raised to show peace. His blond hair was almost in his right eye, and he looked like a teenage boy.

"I don't do autographs," Junil said, almost closing the door.

"Not even for Seven?"

Junil slightly opened the door again. "Seven killed himself. You're a liar."

"I'll show you my cloud and give you intel. I want to work with you."

"Prove that you're Seven."

The boy crouched down and made a circle on the floor with his finger. The circle glowed red and formed a half-sphere. "Mr. Junil, you didn't get here very long ago. You're probably stressed and that's why you're so cold to me. I can review what happened in a specific area and I can replicate a model of it."

"Come inside, but try anything and you're dead."

Seven walked into Junil's top floor hotel room, which was a sight that he could barely take. Seven never really knew what it was like to live in luxury, despite being an information dealer with his outstanding cloud.

"This place is so cool!" Seven ran across the hotel room.

Kuril's eyes remained glued to the television. "I can't believe Rose has a child in their organization."

"I'm a teenager."

"Same thing."

"I'm almost an adult."

"Okay, so why are you here?" Junil interrupted.

"You drink apple juice out of a wine glass?" Seven continued.

Kuril looked over at Seven, who was observing the entire floor. "That's my apple juice."

"Why do you drink apple juice as an adult?"

"It tastes good."

"Weirdo."

Junil cleared his voice to get Seven's attention. "Why are you here?"

Seven finally looked over at Junil, who didn't look so happy with his slanted eyebrows and overflowing aura. The child-like Rose member looked up to ponder why he came. He had forgotten why he showed up to Junil's hotel room. Suddenly, his eyes lit up.

"I have a plan," Seven spoke, grinning at Junil.

"First of all, why are you against Rose?"

Seven sighed. "They deemed me dead, especially when I was capable of defending myself against you and the blond boy." Seven put his fist in the air and stomped down. "I am a force to be reckoned with!"

"I doubt it," Kuril said. "What's the plan anyways?"

"Let's hold One's girlfriend hostage."

Junil turned to Seven. "James has a girlfriend?"

"Unofficially. They're in love."

"That's smart, but how will we even meet her?"

Seven faked a laugh in order to express his superior intelligence. "I have her information. I met her a few times anyway."

"Why have you met One's girlfriend?" Junil asked.

"She wants to see him really badly and has attempted to contact him through me."

"Where can we meet her?"

"Lucky for you, I already contacted her to meet us at the empty lot where you brutally murdered Nine."

Junil scoffed. "Brutal makes it sound rough."

"It was pretty rough."

"Anyways, does she have a cloud?"

"Not that I know of."

Junil laughed out of nowhere, and Seven joined him. They were simply bonding over nothing except their own intelligence. They had an idea on how to finish off Rose, and using James' own emotions against him was their best bet.

"Let's go." Junil lightly slapped Seven's shoulder. "You should redeem yourself and join the police force after this."

"I'll consider."

Kuril finally spoke up. "I'm not joining you guys. Do this yourself."

Seven kept smiling. "Come on! Lighten up!"

"When did you join Rose?"

Seven looked up as he pondered. "Like two months ago."

"I don't care about you so much then. If you're our ally, be our ally. I'm not getting involved this time."

"Bleh. Let's go, Junil!"

The detective and the informant went through the hotel door. "See you later, Kuril," Junil said before shutting the door behind him.

Junil and Seven went off into the street. Junil hid himself with a beanie and sunglasses. They quickly approached the empty lot by Zipline, where Junil had ended Nine's life. Seven could barely contain his excitement.

"How old are you?" Junil asked.

"Seventeen."

"Yikes."

Junil and Seven made it into the empty lot and saw a girl waiting there. Her black hair matched the monotone background of the building behind her.

"Well?" Abigail said.

"You want to know how to save James, right?" Seven asked, taking charge of his plan.

"Who's this guy with you, Seven?"

"Mr. Junil."

Abigail's eyes widened as Junil's eyes made contact with hers. These were the eyes of a model meeting a ruthless killer who acts in the name of justice, and his next target was her own lover, James.

Abigail tried to become intimidating by experimenting with facial expressions, but failed to do anything to Junil. "You're the one trying to kill James."

"I'm just another killer on the road," Junil replied.

Seven tried to execute his plan as he scripted. "Now then—"

Junil scratched his head. "Seven, you know my cloud ability, correct?"

"I did my research on it."

"Do I try it?"

Abigail knew what was coming. She immediately made an effort to run away, but was only chased by Junil, who used his left hand to immobilize Abigail.

"I have no intention of hurting you," Junil said, "I only wish for you to comply."

Abigail heard his words, but was scared nonetheless. Junil took out his phone and dialed for James. He wanted to make sure James knew his lover was in trouble.

"Hello," Junil said as James picked the phone up.

"Junil," James answered, "something wrong?"

"We have your girlfriend hostage."

James went silent. The anger in his voice was shown in his response. "Where?"

"We're at the empty lot by Zipline. Be there in ten minutes or she dies." Junil hung up the phone.

"While you distract him, I'm going to take his life," Seven said.

"So Abigail and I are the distraction?"

Seven smiled. "You're good at this."

"Let's end this entire war," Junil replied, grinning at the teenage boy.

"We make a great duo."

"If it's really this simple, we can definitely pardon your crimes after we win."

Abigail was being pinned to the dirty ground by Junil, who held his gun to her head. Though she regained the strength to move, she knew that she was helpless in this situation. Seven hid behind a bunch of garbage bags and trash cans, unable to be seen by the normal person. Everything was going to go smoothly.

In almost no time, James walked into the alleyway. He looked at Abigail being pinned onto the ground.

James looked at Junil. "Let Abigail go or Seven dies."

Seven was too shocked to even hold the gun anymore. How would James even know he was there? He was silent and perfectly hidden.

Junil loosened his grip on his gun, but easily tightened it again. "Then I'll kill Abigail—"

James looked directly into Junil's eyes, causing Junil to fall asleep for three seconds. Seven, who couldn't see anything, thought they were having a standoff. Junil immediately woke up after those three seconds and started to scream. He had already dropped his gun and stopped holding Abigail onto the floor. His pupils dilated, his body was shaking, and he couldn't process his thoughts.

"Bastard!" Seven screamed, getting out of his hiding spot, aiming his pistol at James.

James turned his head to Seven and looked into his eyes as well. Seven passed out for three seconds like Junil. When he woke up, he dropped the gun. He started to have a breakdown and showed similar physical symptoms to Junil.

"What did you do?" Abigail asked, standing up and gripping onto James' arm.

"I panicked."

"What happened to them?"

"I let them both envision one thousand deaths."

What Junil and Seven had seen was beyond words. Drowning, mutilation, stabbing, you name it. Going through so many of those visions that it became a blur, the duo was startled, barely able to open their eyes. Watching yourself die one thousand times in the span of three seconds gives you barely enough time to process it, but it hits you right when it ends. Three seconds of unbearable pain, fear, and horror flashed right in front of the two.

Abigail slapped James across the face and grabbed his arm. "That's awful! You use your eyes for good!"

"I didn't mean to do that. I panicked."

Abigail quickly let go of James' arm and charged for the gun Junil dropped. She swiped it off the ground and aimed it at Junil's head. He was still on the ground shaking. She fired a bullet, but standing in front of it was James. The bullet hit the wall behind him. The suppressor was still loud for Abigail, who had no experience with firearms.

"I won't let you do that." James looked into Abigail's eyes too. "Adam would get pissed."

Abigail fell asleep, and catching her with his left arm was James. She dropped Junil's gun, which James kicked away. He called Adam to help pick him up with his time stopping ability. Carrying an unconscious woman around Velindas would certainly attract police attention.

As Adam arrived on the scene, he saw what happened. While stopping time, if Adam held onto a person, they'd go into a state of stopped time as well if he so wished. He intended on utilizing such an ability so James could get away and bring Abigail to safety.

Junil got to his feet and covered his glasses. "What the hell did I just see, James?"

"I'm sorry. I panicked."

"Dear God, please tell me the girl isn't hurt."

"She's dreaming about some fantasies of hers. I gave her the good end of the stick."

Junil leaned against the wall in the empty lot and caught his breath. "You're a monster."

"I'm sorry."

"I'll see you later, Junil," Adam said, focusing on getting James home.

Junil stood there with his plans foiled. Seven was still crouched over trying to comprehend such a cloud and every death he lived. They lost. Their magnificent plan was foiled so easily just by James' presence. He was a league above them. He couldn't be stopped. It was a breaking point in Junil's hope.

"Adam, wait," Junil said, trying to stop him.

"By the way, Junil, I like your new glasses." Adam faced away from Junil. "Copycat."

Instantaneously, William appeared with a sword conjured from his own fire pointed at James. Junil and Seven watched as the third head of Rose tipped his sword at James' chin, being sure to not look him in the eyes. It was clear William knew James' true ability.

"Not so fast, you two."

"Where the hell did you come from?" Adam asked, standing next to James.

"Let's just say that I had a burning flame in the corner of this area. I had plenty of burning flames across the city, all sealed by Twelve's bubbles to not spread a fire."

"How come we didn't see it? How could Twelve's cloud be used beyond death?"

"It was a very small flame, which was hidden right by the trash cans in the corner. I'm surprised the kid didn't see it." William intentionally dodged the question about Kyra.

James snapped his fingers as the rest of his body didn't move an inch. That was the signal for Adam to make a move.

Adam reappeared behind William with a switchblade, looking to jab it into the side of his head. "You seem to forget I can stop time."

"Kyra!" William screamed as he started to move to face Adam.

A pink hue encased William entirely as Adam closed in on William's head. Due to the pink bubble blanketing William, he could not hold his sword made of his own fire. As the switchblade made contact with William, it broke. Everyone watched in astonishment as the pink hue acted as an invincible shield.

"Down for two more seconds!" William yelled as the shield around him dropped.

With his hands free, William recreated his sword of fire and stabbed Adam in his stomach. "Flames, unlock!"

"Adam!" cried out Junil, who darted toward his best friend.

"Adam…" James watched as his friend was stabbed right in front of him. It was one of the few times he was truly shocked.

Before Junil could reach Adam and William, he was slammed into the ground by a force from above. Making a grand reveal was none other than Mia, who pinned Junil to the dirty lot. The sword was taken out of Adam.

"Stay put." Mia spoke, watching the ongoing fight. "Trust me."

The pink hue surrounded William again. "Go ahead and stop time, Adam. I am invincible when Twelve is hidden."

Adam fell to his knees and hit the ground. "You clever bastard, Three."

"Either we hear about the Blooming Day and what it is…" William looked at James in his eyes.

"Or you're going to let Two die?"

"Exactly."

James refused to speak.

"I have been watching from the back this entire time. I knew what was happening pretty quickly, but I had to act accordingly."

"What do you mean?"

"When you kill another cloud user, your cloud grows stronger. When the Rose killers take down Rose, you're going to kill both of them for your own gain, James. I could never establish Adam's motive, but seeing as he's your ally, I had to take him out. I know what you want, James."

"What do I want?" James asked.

"You have a medical condition that could kill you. Due to the fact that clouds adapt to their user's will, you would be able to survive the life-threatening medical issue at hand if you had enough power. You want to sacrifice Rose to save yourself."

Everyone stared at James.

William chuckled. "I can't believe you'd lie about the Blooming Day and say it was for your sister. I hope you realize that nothing could ever be done for. She's hopeless." William looked over at Adam. "He's not going to live."

"He will."

"You see, James, I am a natural liar. My flames and my cloud is exactly as I said, but did I ever mention that I had an unlock stage? Didn't you realize that I was fully capable of unlocking my cloud this entire time?"

James' eyes widened.

"My cloud unlock…" William put his hand on James' shoulder.

"William…"

"My cloud unlock kills whoever it is used on if a specific condition is met. They must have a part of my fire in them when I unlock my cloud. That person dies within two days, whether you kill me or not."

James didn't move as William's hand stayed on his shoulder.

"If the Rose killers are successful, then you will not be able to save yourself. Both you and Adam will succumb to time."

William, the tan man with a nice-looking blazer and half-slicked back hair, stood before his boss, overpowering him. As James stayed silent, William snickered. "What a shame. Does Adam know that you're using Kaylin as an excuse? Better yet, do you realize that you are now going to die from your own body?"

Abigail woke up, not understanding why more people were joining the scene. Who was this man in a blazer and who was this brunette? She had no clue, as she had never met all of the Rose members. Seeing the gun a few feet away from her, she nonchalantly picked it up as William faced away from her. Everyone except for William took note of her presence as she was the only one actively moving. She placed the gun in her jacket and looked over at the scene in front of her as she put her arms back at her sides.

"James, is this guy in front of you an enemy?"

William turned around. "Who are you?"

"My name is Abigail," she said, putting her hands in her jacket once again.

James interrupted. "He's the reason that Adam is a bloody mess on the floor."

"Are you going to tell me more about the Blooming Day?" William continued talking to James, despite not facing him anymore.

"I can't."

"Then this might get you talking."

As the pink bubble dropped, William darted toward Abigail, recreating a fire sword.

"William, she has a gun!" Mia yelled. "Stop!"

Two bullets fired through the model's jacket as William fell back in his tracks and fell to the ground. James smiled as he watched the second body hit the ground.

Mia watched as William failed to get his second hostage. "Shit," she muttered to herself.

William's face suddenly shifted expression as his eyes widened and his jaw opened. Falling to the ground, William grabbed onto the initial bullet wound as he bled out from his right side. Abigail took the gun out of her jacket and shot him once more, missing her spot, yet hitting his arm. Throwing the gun to the side, Abigail looked over at Adam's body on the ground, then back at James. With the last vision being James' smile, Abigail fainted.

"Thirteen, I suggest you leave along with wherever Twelve is hiding. I have no clue if Three will be okay or not. I think he will. We'll be taking our leave now," James spoke.

Seven finally found his voice amidst the chaos. "What about Two?"

"I ask that you treat him, Seven. I'd be in your debt." James got on his knees and bowed his head.

"Y-Yeah." Seven was clearly complying out of fear, despite James' advances for peace.

Seven walked over to Adam and flipped him over. Creating a sphere around his torso, he replicated what Adam's body was like immediately before he was stabbed.

Adam opened his eyes very easily, almost as if he were fake sleeping. "Thanks, Seven. I owe you one." He scratched the back of his head.

"No problem," he replied.

James reached his hand out to help Adam stand up. Getting on his own two feet with ease, he brushed the dust off himself as he walked over toward Mia.

"Junil looks pretty cute being pinned under someone," Adam joked.

"You look pretty cute with a fucking hole in your stomach," replied the detective.

"Cold."

"Hot," Junil continued, "like the flame that pierced you."

Adam put his hands in his jacket. "You know, Thirteen, I

was going to ask you to get off Junil, but you can stay on him if you want."

"Oh, yeah." Mia stood up.

Junil got on his two feet and stretched his body out. In front of him were his enemies, yet it seemed like no one was fighting him. It was almost as if Rose was at war with itself.

"James, can we go?" Adam asked.

James grabbed Adam's shoulder. "Adam, Three betrayed us. He had a cloud unlock this entire time and it will kill you in approximately two days."

"I don't care. Can we go?"

"Ah, of course."

James picked up Abigail and placed her on his back as Adam grabbed James' hand. The duo was going to leave the scene so casually and easily, despite the brilliance of the plan devised by Seven and Junil. Walking out of the alleyway, the two heads of Rose were unscathed.

Junil, Mia, and Seven watched as they left, knowing they wouldn't be able to beat the tyrants that were Adam and James. Silence filled the empty alleyway as blood slowly dripped from William's body.

"That's it, huh?" Mia asked.

Junil looked over at Mia, who was clearly not paying attention to anyone. "Did Three really have a cloud unlock?"

"He did. He sacrificed himself to take down the ones behind Rose's fall." Mia crouched down and looked at William, who was dying and unconscious. "He isn't going to live."

"Are you implying that both One and Two are pulling the strings behind Kuril and I?"

"That's what William thought."

Junil joined Mia as she stared at William's body. "It's a shame how his plan resulted in his death."

"If he was more careful—"

"No," Junil interrupted, "Two would have still defeated him."

"You might be right. That guy is intelligent beyond belief."

"Only I can take him down."

"Are you saying that you're able to outsmart him?"

Junil looked over at the entrance of the alleyway. "No."

"Then how would you defeat Two?"

Junil stared at his right hand. "I wish I knew."

"One and Two are both unbeatable by any human being."

"Was William just an example of that?"

Mia stood up and started to walk toward the alleyway entrance. "From what I can assume, you and Adam are going to face off eventually."

"It's inevitable."

"You won't be able to do it alone."

"Are you going to help me?"

"No."

Junil sighed. "Thanks."

"I wish you the best of luck."

"I assumed you hated me."

"Don't flatter yourself," she replied, "I still don't like you."

"You didn't say that you hate me."

"I hate you."

"Reminding you only made it worse."

Mia chuckled. "I'm going to go meet up with Twelve again."

"I'll see you around."

"I'll see you soon."

Mia walked out of the alleyway as Junil walked over to Seven. Seven looked up at the grown man with defeat in his eyes.

"Can't beat yourself up, Seven."

"I thought it would work."

"Not every plan is going to work."

The young boy clenched his fists and looked down. "I wish I had more power."

"Why?"

"Because then I could save William right now. I'm just out of energy."

Junil smiled. "You'll be stronger one day."

"I want to be stronger now!" he cried. "I want to save William!"

Junil looked down at William's body. "You can't save everybody. Seems like both of us learned the hard way."

Seven's tears rolled down his face as William's blood decelerated across the lot, going in little patterns along the ground's texture. Junil grabbed the young man and hugged him, stroking his hair.

"Why? Why couldn't I save him? Why am I so weak?"

Junil stared at the empty wall in the lot as he listened to Seven's sobbing. "There was once someone I couldn't save, Seven."

"What was it like?" he asked.

"I couldn't get over it. It was my former assistant. He died in a standoff we had against a group of thugs. I could have saved him if I was stronger then."

"Why is it like this?"

"The world tears people away all the time. We can't always save people. All that matters is if we try."

Seven didn't respond. He took himself out of Junil's embrace and started to tread across the lot. He slumped himself out of the alleyway.

"Hey, Seven," Junil called out.

Looking back, Seven tilted his head as his way of asking what Junil wanted.

"Let's cooperate in the future, okay?"

Continuing to walk out of the alleyway, Seven smiled—a smile that Junil could not see. "Yeah, let's work together again." That smile quickly became a frown again.

Within minutes of real time, Adam and James ended up back at the apartment Abigail stayed at. It was somewhat rundown, but many buildings on the business side of the city are similar to that. Abigail, who was on James' back, slowly opened her eyes.

"I'm headed out," Adam said, walking away.

James made sure to show his appreciation for the getaway. "Thanks, Adam."

"It might be best to stay the night with her," Adam replied, smirking, "if you know what I mean."

"I'll be sure to keep her company."

The time-stopping criminal let out a chuckle. "You never catch hints."

"I caught it, but I don't care for it."

"She loves you."

"I can't stain her with my presence."

Adam took his time to find a response. Unable to convey how he felt about such a phrase, he gave up. "See you back at operations."

"Ah, wait."

Adam turned around. "What is it, captain?"

"I thought I told you not to call me that. I'm not your captain."

Adam scoffed. "I was being friendly."

James sighed. "Can you pick up Kaylin for me?"

Adam pushed his glasses closer to his eyes. "Haven't had action in a long time. I'd love to."

"Don't make a big scene."

"Such little trust in me. I'll be just fine."

James looked away. "Alright."

"Bye-bye!" Adam walked away into the stairwell instead of taking the elevator.

"Abby, you awake?" James asked.

"Yeah."

"Can I have your keys?"

"Oh, sure."

Abigail got off of James' back and onto her own feet. She reached into her pocket and took out her keys, ignoring what James said about himself to Adam. She placed the keys in James' hands, looking up to see his smile. It looked fake to her. Abigail believed she knew James the best, so it was only natural for her to be suspicious of some smiles he makes.

"Thanks," James said, unlocking the door.

"What's wrong, James?"

James walked into her apartment. "Please make tonight the best night of my life."

Abigail bowed her head and followed him, closing the door behind her. "Why are you always hiding things from me?" Her fists clenched.

James was still wearing his smile. "I want you to make me happy, even if it's only for one night."

"Why? Why can't you just let me help you?"

"It's because I love you—"

"Enough of that bullshit!" she screamed. Her face was red, her eyes were watering up, and all she could do was try to hide it.

"Abby."

"What is it?"

"I'm sorry."

"I just want to be of use to you."

A few raindrops hit the apartment window. In Velindas, it almost never rained, but tonight was the night that it did. It wasn't much rain, but it was enough to have people going outside preaching a miracle. It was dark out, and only the city lights from outside could illuminate the raindrops on the window. The two could hear the raindrops hit the window.

James put his hand on her shoulder. "Please make me happy, that's all I want."

"Can I even do that?"

"Can you try?"

Abigail wiped her eyes and looked up. "I'll do my best."

Though he had to lean down, he made sure his lips met hers. All Abigail ever wanted was James, and now she had him. James, who was so goal-oriented, wanted Abigail too, but he couldn't bring himself to put aside his aspirations. Now, for the first time in years, their lips would touch. James was taking control, but Abigail just let him do as he pleased.

Time was frozen between the two, yet Abigail's stomach was full of butterflies. She wanted to make sure James was satisfied, and he was going to make sure that he was getting all he wanted: Abigail's affection. Their hearts were pounding harder than they ever felt once before. James' arms wrapped around Abigail's waist as they locked each other in embrace. James drew his lips back and looked into her eyes. He wanted so much more than a kiss: he wanted to be selfish.

James kept his eyes locked in with hers, almost as if he was analyzing her face. "I'm really greedy."

"You can have all you want tonight," she quavered, slightly moving her head to the side.

James bit down on her neck and redirected her to the bed she always slept on, forcing her against the mattress. Their bodies were only growing steamier, but every time they touched, they would find a way to go even beyond that heat. James continued to keep his mouth focused on her neck, marking it as his. He wanted to leave a bruise on her neck so she could remember she was his whenever she saw herself. Abigail let out a few whimpers as he kept himself on her, but James didn't care. He was selfish.

"It's getting hot in here," James said, standing up and taking off his coat.

Abigail took off her shirt while still on the bed, revealing a black bra underneath. She slid off her black leggings, revealing the second piece to her outfit. James was smiling as he looked down on her.

"I'm going to know your entire body," he barely let out.

Abigail didn't know what to say.

James took his black t-shirt off, revealing a body formed from malnutrition and fitness. He was strong, but he was more toned than buff. He slid his black dress pants off and found himself in bed with her. Laying next to each other, Abigail's back faced

James' torso. He started to feel her with his somewhat twitchy hands. He wanted to know everything from her legs to her head. James wanted to just let himself go. James continued to slide his hands across her body.

James put his mouth close to her ear. "I'm the happiest man in the world right now," he said, his breath steaming against her ear.

She turned around to face James and started to feel his body. As much as James wanted her, she wanted him. She was growing addicted to his touch, something she craved for so long. Her hand met James' messy black hair, and slid down his face. Her hands felt his sides, his waist, and his chest. She leaned into his face.

"I'm selfish too."

She kissed him, satisfying the urge to make out for the second time. Her hands glided across his body and his hands did the same for hers. Sometimes James' finger would poke at the underwear she was wearing, but sometimes his hands would reach her hair. James moved his finger to the mark he made earlier. He was confident this was going to leave a bruise.

"Can we stay like this all night?" James asked.

"I want to stay like this forever," Abigail replied, turning herself to signal him.

James put his arm around her body and rested. He didn't respond. He closed his eyes and moved his head to her hair, where he passed out.

Taking notice, Abigail smiled, trying to hold back her laugh. "Of course you pass out in a time like this. You must've been so exhausted."

All James wanted was to stay there with Abigail forever, but the reality was looming over him: the Blooming Day was tomorrow. He fell asleep smiling as Abigail laid down with him, trying not to fall asleep, but rather embrace her lover.

Abigail stroked James' hair. "I'll take care of you. I promise." It wouldn't be long before the both of them were asleep together, bodies pressed as one, united for what both of them feared was the last time.

The red-lensed criminal walked into the Velindas hospital casually. Looking both ways, he saw plenty of people waiting and a front desk. With his hands in his pockets, Adam approached the front desk, hoping to get Kaylin quick and easy.

"I'm looking for Kaylin."

"Excuse me, sir, but we need a full name for the patient you're looking for and some identification from you."

"I have to show some kind of ID?"

The lady working at the front desk sighed. "Yes."

"I don't have an identity. Can I please take that Kaylin girl?"

"I'm sorry, but I can't help you then."

Adam groaned. "You guys suck."

Adam walked over to the two big doors leading into the actual hospital itself and opened them. People watched him walk in with no care, but the front desk crew immediately scrambled after him.

"Sir," the lady spoke again from behind, "you can't be in here."

"I'm picking someone up."

"You have to leave or I'm calling the cops." She grabbed onto his arm.

Adam stopped walking and turned his head over to the woman. "You have three seconds to take your hand off me or I'll kill you."

In fear, she let go of Adam, who continued walking on as the front desk crew watched. They rushed back into the waiting area and immediately dialed for the police. The people in the waiting room talked amongst themselves amidst the chaos, not knowing what was happening.

Casually walking past doctors and nurses, Adam traversed the hospital. After realizing he had no clue which room Kaylin was in, he decided to go into the doctors' lounge. Walking into the room, he was the only one not dressed professionally, which gave him weird stares.

"Are you supposed to be here?" a doctor asked.

"I'm looking for a patient."

"I'm sorry, but you can't be back here." The doctor stood up to redirect him out of the room, but Adam was not cooperative.

Adam shoved the doctor aside and noticed a desk with a few controls on them. "Oh! Is this the loudspeaker control thing?"

Another doctor got in front of Adam, but she was also shoved aside. More doctors would try jumping in as Adam got closer to the loudspeaker controls, but they were all pushed off. None of them would try to tackle Adam, only restrict him. Either way, it wouldn't have worked. Adam observed the controls and grinned, trying to figure out which button did what.

Pressing a button, Adam finally got his chance to locate Kaylin. "You know who you are, darling. Walk over to the waiting room and meet me there. Thank you!"

From her hospital room, Kaylin heard the loudspeakers and broke into a cold sweat. She immediately unhooked herself from the hospital equipment in a scramble and got up, nearly falling over.

A doctor walked into the girl's room. "Kaylin, you have to stay put. There is an unwanted intruder."

"I'm the one he wants, Dr. Shukar."

He attempted to play a voice of reason to her. "We can't just give you to an intruder."

"That man has the power to kill anyone he wants. If you don't let me go, he'll kill you first."

Dr. Shukar froze as Kaylin walked past him. "Kaylin—"

"Did you forget I'm blind? Bring me to the waiting room."

"Who is this intruder?"

"I can't tell you who he is."

"What is he like?"

Kaylin's heart started to pound. "He's a crow. He is no different from a bad omen. He's a sign of bad luck. Whenever you see him, you know someone is going to suffer or die soon. He's evil—and once you think you have any hope, he watches it die and feasts on it right in front of you."

"You must know this man very well."

Kaylin started to shiver. "I do."

"I won't let him hurt you—"

She cut the doctor off. "You don't understand. He isn't going to hurt me. He's going to hurt anyone who tries to come between me and him right now."

"What does he want with you?"

She touched Dr. Shukar's arm in an attempt to grab his hand. "Please bring me to him. I don't want anyone innocent getting hurt."

Dr. Shukar grabbed Kaylin's hand. "Can I trust that you'll be safe?"

"Yes."

"Then follow me."

The doctor and Kaylin walked to the waiting room. There were doctors and nurses scrambling trying to figure out what chaos was happening in the medical center. As the two opened the hospital doors that led into the waiting room, they were met by Adam's turned back as he held his hands in the air. In front of him, police were grouped up trying to close the distance.

"The police are already here?" Dr. Shukar asked.

Kaylin realized what was happening. "Get away from him!" Kaylin screamed as she let go of the doctor's hand and ran forward.

"Now, now. Let's not play rough. It's clear my hostage doesn't want violence." Adam looked over at Kaylin, who had accidentally bumped into him. He put his arm over her shoulder. "See? She clearly wants to come with me. Isn't that right?"

Dr. Shukar noticed Kaylin's trembling. He had finally understood what Kaylin was talking about. Kaylin had some sense of hope of being able to reunite with Junil after being discharged, but the man in the brown coat killed it, and now he's toying around with his prey.

"Yes." Kaylin gulped. "I want to go with this man. Please let us leave."

An officer butted in. "Sorry, but you can't just do that. We need an official discharge from the hospital and we need this man to show some identification."

Adam smiled. "Five."

Kaylin froze.

And his smile grew bigger. "Four."

"Please, let us through!" Kaylin yelled out. "You don't understand!"

"Three."

The senior officer aimed at Adam, soon being joined by the other officers. "Why are you counting down?"

"Two."

Kaylin started screaming at the top of her lungs. "Please let us go, you'll all die!"

"One."

In an instant, all the officers in front of Adam died. Kaylin heard several gunshots and multiple bodies hit the floor as Dr. Shukar watched in horror. Adam had stopped time and shot each officer—all with their respective handguns. Adam was standing behind the bodies. Dr. Shukar was the only one in the room who could see what was happening, as everyone else was already evacuated. Adam walked over the bodies and grabbed Kaylin's right shoulder.

He crouched down to whisper into her left ear. "What a shame."

Kaylin fell onto her knees crying.

"By the way, Dr. Shukar, you are Junil's physician and doctor, correct?" Adam stood up straight, reading the doctor's name tag.

"Y-Yes."

"I like the glasses you gave him. Very similar to the red lenses that I have."

Dr. Shukar didn't respond.

The criminal crouched back down and grabbed Kaylin's hand, picking her up onto her feet. "Let's go, okay?"

Kaylin had no response.

Adam walked out of the waiting room holding Kaylin's hand as Dr. Shukar watched. He eventually fell to his knees too after watching the two of them leave.

"That man is a crow," he muttered to himself.

Adam brought Kaylin over to the base of operations, which was so hidden that the police had never been able to spot it. In order to avoid the cops, Adam had to stop time whenever he could and make pauses in the alleyways. It was inconvenient, but he was okay with it.

He directed Kaylin onto a nice-looking couch in their base. She laid down on the couch, exhausted and overwhelmed. Standing over her was a predator—one that she could sense without seeing him.

The crow-like man smiled. "Welcome home, Kaylin."

CHAPTER IX

The very next day, James walked into the base of operations, greeted by the sight of Kaylin and Adam.

"What's up, James?"

"Let's play some cards before the day begins."

Adam hopped off his chair. "Oh, fun!"

Taking a seat at the table, James let out a deep breath and relaxed himself. Adam started to tap the table with his finger, creating a melody. The head of Rose took the pack of cards that was already sitting on the table and started to shuffle the deck.

"The Blooming Day is today, James."

James didn't look at Adam. "I know."

"Are you ready?"

"I've been ready my entire life."

Adam slammed his fist on the table. "Then let's shake the world with our final push!"

"Quite the enthusiasm," James replied. "Take your cards."

Grabbing his cards, Adam started to play his game of war with

James. "Keeping my head up even when it's hard is something I excel at."

James looked at Adam. "You're ready for your end of the Blooming Day?"

"Of course."

"I'd love to see this happen."

"I should be saying that."

Slamming down another set of cards, Adam revealed a joker, while James revealed a king. Taking the two cards and putting them in a separate pile, Adam smiled as he was already winning.

"The king has a king." Adam laughed.

James looked over at his friend. "I didn't know we were playing with jokers."

Adam groaned. "Doesn't matter, I won this round."

"Kaylin, you know we have to go soon, right?" James asked, looking at the blind girl sitting alone.

"Why can't you accept that I just want to live life normally?"

James didn't care for her words. "We're going to the office building by the end of Closedown Avenue soon. Please prepare yourself."

Adam interrupted the conversation. "War!"

Adam slammed down his card, but James did not. In fact, James was staring over at Kaylin the entire time. Taking a glance at James' face, he noticed a solemn expression overcoming the leader of Rose. His comrade felt enveloped in a deep despair and he wondered if the meeting with Abigail had anything to do with it.

"I'm headed out for a bit," Adam spoke up, catching James' attention.

"Why?"

Pushing back his red lenses, he turned away from James and headed toward the exit of the building they were hiding in. "I just remembered that I have to do something."

James stood up and grabbed Adam's shoulder. "Please, I want

to talk to you for a little longer. We both don't know what can happen out there."

Without turning, Adam's voice turned contemplative, a rare sight for both James and Kaylin. "You and I will definitely see each other again. I know you're scared, but we'll be okay."

James began to tear up as his grip on Adam's shoulder weakened. Turning around, Adam hugged the black-haired man. The two men, who had such contrasting features, complimented each other perfectly. James dug his head into Adam's shoulder and began to sob. Adam brushed his hair with his hand and shushed him.

"It will be okay. It's okay to be scared. You'll see me again."

The head of Rose's cries grew louder as he started to muffle his screaming sobs into Adam's jacket. As Adam continued to stroke James' hair, he noticed Kaylin listening in, almost feeling empathetic for her cold brother.

"I'm so scared, Adam," James muttered.

Adam smiled, even though James could not see it. "It's okay."

"I hate this. I hate living like this. I hate this so much, Adam."

"You are the most pure being to ever touch the face of the Earth, James."

"I hate this."

"I wonder…"

James finally looked up to Adam. His eyes and face were red after sobbing on Adam's brown coat. "What, Adam?"

"Did I ease your pain at least a little bit?"

"Yeah."

"I don't have long to live." Adam looked up at the ceiling.

"I promise you that everything we have done won't be in vain. Kaylin will see glory."

Adam backed up and bowed his head. "Thank you."

"No, thank you."

Regaining his stature, Adam turned around again. "It's been fun, James. I'll see you tonight?"

"What do you want to do?"

"Let's go see that cat again later. I'd love to spend my last days around life."

James sniffled. "Yeah."

"May God bless your soul, James. You will be okay and so will I." Adam put his hand on the doorknob and twisted it. "I love you, okay?"

"I love you too."

Adam left the building for what James feared was the last time. James was always a scared person and it was up to Adam to reassure him, but this time he felt scared even with Adam's gentle touch. James looked over to Kaylin, who listened in on the whole thing.

"I'm sorry about that," he spoke.

"What's going on?"

"Adam doesn't have much longer to live. I don't know when he will die."

"What happened?"

James walked over to Kaylin. "Three betrayed us."

"I'm sorry to hear about Adam."

"Kaylin, I want to give you a switchblade for self-defense."

The blind individual looked toward James' voice. "Why?"

James looked away. "It will help you during the Blooming Day."

"I won't have to kill anybody, right?"

"No, it'll probably be used for rope."

Kaylin smiled. "Thank you."

Back at the hotel, Kuril woke up on the couch to see Junil sitting on the bed watching the news at low volume.

"Good morning, Junil."

"Good morning."

"How was the fight with Five? I never got to ask." Kuril asked.

Junil had no expression. "It was hard. Five really wanted to kill me, so her death was somewhat brutal."

"I could imagine. Weren't you guys friends?"

"Yeah, I never wanted to kill her," Junil lied.

"On my end, James and I had some weird talk."

"What was it?"

"James' true cloud is the ability to make his opponent see things just by looking into their eyes. It's deadly."

"What did he make you see?" Junil asked.

Kuril started to stretch. "He lied about his cloud. He told me his cloud allowed him to replicate pain, so if I shot him, I'd kill Kaylin."

"Did you shoot him?"

"It was an illusion, but I didn't."

"Why would he do that?"

Kuril looked over at Junil. "He wanted to test how loyal I was to Kaylin's life."

"Odd."

"I think he's planning something."

"I know Rose has a plan, but I don't know what it is."

Kuril walked over to Junil and got on one knee. Junil, who was sitting on the edge of his bed, had no idea what was happening.

"Thank you for everything, Junil."

"I'm just doing my job."

Kuril stood up and sat next to Junil on the edge of the bed.

"How many Rose deaths are reported?" Kuril asked.

"All of them except the final two, who are still alive."

"Final stretch, let's make it count."

Junil looked over to Kuril. "One of us probably won't make it."

"We both know this is risky."

"You're like the brother I never had, Kuril. This last week with you has been one for the ages."

"No matter what happens between us, we'll always be brothers."

The two men had formed an unbreakable bond in the span of a week. There was nothing that could separate them besides death, and they wanted to make sure it stayed that way. The goal was simple: Rose was going down, but they didn't want to lose each other.

Junils phone started to ring.

"Pick it up," Kuril said.

Junil answered the call. "Hello?"

"Hey, Junil."

"Adam?"

"Don't you think it's time for the final stretch?"

"I don't want to do this, Adam."

Junil could hear Adam chuckle behind the phone. "You'll be fine. We have to meet up and fight eventually. I think that should be today."

"Adam, you're a great person. You don't understand how much I don't want to fight."

"We have to."

"Please, Adam."

"Show up to the same spot where Twelve died at noon. Bring no one else."

"I refuse."

"Failure to comply won't help."

"Adam—"

The call ended. Junil sat there in silence, barely gripping his phone in his right hand. He stood up slowly, then immediately threw his phone into the ground. Kuril only watched.

"Prepare yourself, Junil. Reality is hitting hard today."

Junil stood still. "I know."

"Do you know what Adam has planned?"

"I hope it isn't what I think it is."

Kuril's eyes looked around the room. In the small amount of time he interacted with Adam, he had already figured out his character. Adam's plan was going to be a simple one, but it would prove fatal to Junil.

"Don't let your emotions take over, Junil."

"I'll try."

The two were frozen in time. Junil started to move again and headed toward the door. His body dragged itself across the room as he approached the exit.

"Heading over early?" Kuril asked.

Junil didn't look back. "I know Adam is there early."

"Good luck, Junil."

"Thanks."

The door opened and closed. Kuril sat alone in Junil's hotel room, watching the television. He was staring off into the light the television sent to his eyes, but he didn't feel any of it. All he could do is imagine Junil's pain, but even that was difficult for him.

Junil's death march started as he walked down Velindas. The bustling city around him was highlighted by the tourists, the prostitutes, the stores, and the wannabe gangs consisting of teenagers. Junil didn't care anymore. Justice was no longer his priority—Adam was.

Everything in Junil's life wouldn't be there if it wasn't for Adam's sacrifice. Junil didn't carry his pistol to battle. His hands, which were stained with the blood of countless people in the name of justice, didn't want to take Adam's life.

"Hey, watch where you're going!" a man called out to Junil after colliding with him.

"I'm sorry."

Junil couldn't think or walk straight. All he could focus on was Adam and his motives. What was Adam's part in the Blooming Day? Junil's head flowed with a stream of questions, none of which could be answered.

A kid walked up to Junil. "Hey, are you Junil?"

"If I was?"

"Are you?"

"I am."

"Mr. Junil, I'm going to be like you one day!"

Junil faked a smile. "I never saw a kid idolize me."

"Is detective work hard?"

"It's hard," Junil replied, "it's really hard."

"One day, I'll make it big like you!"

"Listen, kid. I'll promise you one thing: Rose is going down."

The kid's face brightened up as if Junil said a signature line. "Thank you, Mr. Junil!"

"Are you lost?"

"Yeah."

"Is there somewhere I should bring you?"

"Do you know where Kibbler Street is?"

"I'll lead you there."

Junil started to walk alongside the child, who was very open with the detective by his body language alone. The kid really liked the detective for some reason Junil couldn't follow. Junil was looking ahead, not paying attention to whether the kid was next to him or not.

Kibbler Street was not very far away from where the two met. While the child was frolicking next to Junil, the detective was pondering.

"We're here," Junil said, returning to reality.

The kid ran up to the brunette in black, who slapped a one hundred dollar bill into the hand of the little boy. He ran off with the money as fast as he could.

"What's up, Junil?"

"I'm not very surprised." The detective sighed. "Kids don't know modern detectives."

The girl sighed as well. "I wanted to meet up with you."

"I thought you didn't want to talk, Mia."

"Now I want to talk to you."

"About what?"

Mia looked at Junil up and down, then signalled him to start walking with her. Junil and Mia ended up side by side, feet moving on one of the many streets in Velindas. Though the sky was cloudy and no stars were in sight, the business side of Velindas was always lit up. In fact, all of Velindas was always bright.

"What are you doing today?" Mia asked.

"Two already asked me to meet up with him to fight." Junil replied.

Mia looked at Junil while walking. His face was neutral, unreadable, and deadly. "The Blooming Day, of course."

"This is apart of his plan?"

"I assume so."

Junil kept walking, but his mind froze. He needed to keep pace with Mia. "Explain what the Blooming Day is," Junil said, adjusting his glare to Mia, "or I'll kill you."

Mia sighed. "I don't know anything about it."

"Why do you want to talk to me?"

"I wanted to help you take down Two."

Junil paused the conversation for a few seconds to think. "Why?"

"If Two wants Rose gone, that means both Twelve and I would be in danger."

"You're trying to protect yourselves?"

"He's threatening." Mia continued walking along the road with Junil. "He can kill me."

"I see."

Mia pointed ahead. "Do you know where you're meeting up with him?"

"The abandoned church."

Junil knew the city by heart. If someone needed help going anywhere, he could always just show them the way to their destination. Born and raised in Velindas, Junil became very well accustomed to the streets, the paths, and even the alleyways and where they led. Though he never knew where Rose was located, he knew just about every building and the purpose it had for the city. During the walk with Mia, he noticed they were walking on a path that would lead them to Adam and Junil's meeting point: the abandoned church Twelve died in.

"Mia," Junil said, breaking the silence, "are you escorting me to Adam?"

"It was by sheer coincidence that we were already on the way," she replied.

Junil sighed. "You plan on being there during our meeting, correct?"

"I'm going to help you kill him."

"Why are you so easygoing around me? Have you not considered that I may attack you?" Junil interrogated the woman standing next to him.

Mia looked over at him. "I trust you."

Junil collected his thoughts, but was unable to reach any conclusions regarding the Blooming Day. "Tell me all you know about the Blooming Day."

"It's a plan created by Adam and James. That is really all I know."

"I see."

"We're almost there."

"You know, we're half-siblings. It's neat to fight alongside the daughter of my father."

Mia blew the air out of her lungs almost as if she were smoking a cigarette. "I suppose I can empathize with the fact that you grew up with that bastard."

"He wasn't there in my life."

"I see."

"Let's win this battle together."

Junil had been through a lot: fights, gunshot wounds, jabs, slices, black eyes, but he had never been on such a level of pain mentally to where it was incomparable to any physical pain. His brain was on fire, but it was too much for anyone to understand. Velindas' favorite detective was going through so much more pain than just the battle wounds from Rose members, he was taking the mental strain of knowing he had to face his friend one final time.

As he took his final steps toward the end of the street, he knew the church was just one turn away. Junil's heart started to race as his mouth grew dry. He didn't know what Adam was going to say or do, but he had a hint that someone would die. His muscles tightened up and the detective was overcome with a cold feeling across his body.

"We're here." Mia looked at Junil. "You look pale."

"I'm just nervous."

"I would be too."

Junil started to slowly inch toward the church entrance. "Let's go."

Mia took the chance to speak up. "I'm going to surprise attack him. You just have to keep him at bay."

"I see. What if he stops time?"

"Stop him first. I know about your cloud."

"Okay."

Junil only felt worse by those words, but he knew facing Adam was inevitable. He opened the door to see an empty church with a tan male praying at the church pew. The door closed behind him, and it was the loudest slam he had ever heard from a door. Junil walked in and leaned against the church pew adjacent to the one Adam was praying at.

Adam finished his prayer by touching his head, then both of his shoulders, then his heart. The second-in-command head of Rose was always religious, but never let it consume his daily life. Adam did in fact believe in God and his holiness, but he was still a ruthless killer.

"Still religious?" Junil asked behind Adam.

"I just needed God."

Junil exhaled. "For what?"

"Just a big day."

"What's the deal?"

Adam stood up and walked over to a table that stood in the middle of the nave of the church. "It had to catch your eye when you walked in. We're going to be playing chess."

"What's the point?"

Adam gave a small laugh and smiled. "We're going to gamble with each other's lives."

Junil froze. Not even looking at the chess board, he responded, "If I win, you die?"

"And if I win, you die."

Junil started to sweat profusely. The perspiration was practically dripping down his face as his body became cold. He knew Adam could sense his fear, but when he finally tilted his head over to see Adam, he was only met with the withdrawn, teasing, and cruel expression that haunted Velindas.

"Take a seat, Junil," Adam said, sitting down first.

Junil slowly followed after and sat down.

"White always goes first," Adam spoke.

Junil opened the game by moving his center pawn. Adam immediately responded by moving his pawn in return. Junil put his knight on the frontlines with his cold, sweaty hand.

"Sicilian Defense isn't going to work on me, Junil." Adam moved his other pawn.

Junil's heart began to pound more than it ever has. Adam was stellar at chess. In fact, Adam had never lost a chess match in his life. Junil, growing up with the criminal, knew very well that Adam was a chess prodigy.

Junil gulped as he moved another piece. "We couldn't have played a game I'm good at too?"

"You're pretty good at chess." Adam moved his piece swiftly.

"Not as much as you."

"I'm flattered," Adam replied.

"I don't want to do this, Adam."

Adam's eyes gazed into Junil's eyes. "Did you really think you had any hope against me?" Adam moved his piece without looking.

The chess board was cluttered with pieces, each one holding more value than just being a pawn or a knight. These were the pieces that defined someone's life.

"Adam, why did you become a criminal?"

Adam kept playing instead of responding.

"Maybe things would have worked out. Maybe you didn't have to be a runaway," Junil continued. "Why?"

"Checkmate in four moves."

Junil immediately felt a wave of unease over him. He felt like puking his guts out. He felt worse than sick. The detective's head was spinning as his vision faded. Junil hesitantly moved his piece, trying to read Adam's dead face to see what move would be best.

Adam moved his queen. Junil tried gaining time, but succumbed to moving his piece. Adam placed his bishop closer to Junil's frontlines immediately. Junil was running out of time for his moves. He tried pushing a random move with his queen in hopes it would throw Adam off. Adam chuckled and moved his queen closer. Junil realized it was hopeless at that point. In the next move, it was going to be checkmate. Junil moved his queen in to hopefully prevent it, but even he could see the opening in his defense.

"It was a fun match, Junil."

Adam put the tip of his index finger on his own king and knocked it over. It felt like forever, but Junil had finally watched Adam's king fall.

The criminal smiled. "I resign. Good game."

"What?" Junil looked up at Adam, who stood up to stretch his legs.

Adam slammed his gun on the chess board. Chess pieces hit the floor and rolled across the board. "Guess you have to kill me."

"Adam, why would you surrender?"

From behind Adam, a figure appeared, enveloped in a pink bubble. Launching itself at him, Adam quickly turned around, seeing that the figure was none other than Mia.

Instead of stopping Adam's ability to stop time, Junil failed to react as he pondered on Adam's decision. At the same time,

Adam failed to react, getting pinned onto the floor before being able to stop time.

Adam reappeared at the apse of the church. "Bad choice."

Mia stood up and turned around to see Adam a few meters away from him, clearly unhappy with the assault that was conducted on him. His usual smile wasn't showing, and instead, contempt filled his eyes.

Adam scoffed. "The same fucking pink bubble shit. I should have killed you and your little girlfriend. Do you think I am so low that I can't fucking get past your shitty bubble strategy?"

"Junil, now!" Mia yelled, signaling him to attack.

Junil jumped out of his seat and activated his left hand while approaching Adam. Adam's eyes looked down on Junil from the apse of the church as he got closer. Instead of dodging, Adam allowed Junil to close that space. It was maybe the biggest threat Junil ever was to Adam.

Before he could touch Adam, Junil reappeared next to Mia with his activated hand on her shoulder, nullifying the power of Kyra's bubble. Mia fell to the ground as blood spilled out of her stomach. In his confusion, Junil noticed a bloody switchblade on the ground. Behind both of them was Adam, who had his back faced away.

"Simple tricks can't fool a man twice."

"Mia!" Junil yelled.

Adam raised his voice. "You can hide, Twelve. If you wish to come out and save Mia, I will let you. However, only on the terms that you two leave Junil and I alone."

In ten seconds, Kyra opened the entrance of the church door, holding a gun that pointed at Adam the second he could see it. Slowly walking forward, Kyra held the gun with two hands as Junil turned his head to see the girl he supposedly shot in the same spot, holding a gun aimed at his best friend.

"You're not experienced with firearms, Twelve," Adam said.

"I'm experienced enough to kill you."

Adam closed the gap between him and Kyra, leaning forward and grabbing the gun, aiming it directly at his head. "Tell me, Twelve. Are you experienced enough to pull the trigger on me? Experienced enough to kill me?"

Kyra's hands started to tremble as Adam's grip on the gun ended up stronger than hers.

"Are you experienced enough to put an end to my life?" Adam smiled.

Kyra's arms began to tremble as well.

"Are you experienced enough to kill the man who devised the Blooming Day plan?"

Kyra fired, yet right as she did, Adam was already behind her, crouching down with his hand on her shoulder and his mouth to ear.

"Pathetic," he whispered in the criminal's ear.

Junil interrupted Adam and Kyra by walking toward the two. "Twelve, you have to save Mia and get out of here."

"What about you?"

"This is a private matter. Save Mia."

She nodded. "Yeah."

Walking over to Mia and encasing her body in a bubble, she quickly picked up the Violet with ease and started to escort her to the church door as Adam and Junil watched. She was surprisingly strong, as most cloud users were.

"I wish you luck, Junil," she said, walking out of the church doors.

As the church doors closed, Junil and Adam turned to each other to make eye contact. The duo, no matter how split apart by affiliations, were always a team. It was about time that one of them had to kill the other because of their destinies.

"I remember," Junil said, "you wanted to become a detective. Why not become one now?"

"Did I perhaps inspire you?"

"You're the reason I'm a detective, Adam. Feel honored."

"What you have right now is not what I wanted."

Junil only got more confused. "I'm one of the world's greatest detectives, what more would you want?"

"I wanted to be the world's greatest detective. No debate about it."

"So what does this mean to me?"

Adam smiled at Junil. It was the most human smile that the man could produce. "I'm going to give you exactly what I wanted."

"You're going to make me the world's best detective?"

"Yes."

"I hope I'm not piecing this together."

"The Blooming Day is the last stand for Rose," Adam said, "and it's going to launch you into first place as the world's greatest. You'll forever be engraved in history."

"I'm going to become number one for taking down Rose?"

"That's exactly correct."

Adam turned around and inched toward the apse of the church, almost as if he were hesitant. Taking the pistol off the table, he tossed the handgun to the detective as he turned around to face him.

Junil cupped his arms to catch Adam's gun. "What's going to happen if this plan fails?"

Adam stared at Junil from the apse of the abandoned church. "My plan is for you to kill me. My will is for you to kill me. There's no other way I'd want to die."

"Even though you know it would be painful for me?"

"You'd gain a lot of power and recognition from it. My cloud is extremely compelling and you would become as powerful as me. Maybe you'd get a cloud unlock from it."

Observing the gun, Junil's vision slightly faded. This gun was going to take the life of his best friend, his lifetime comrade, his partner, but also his enemy. Junil's hands were going to be stained with blood once again, but the mental toll was going to hit him harder than he could ever prepare for.

"Do you think God will forgive me?" Junil asked.

"I'll be your vouch into the gates of heaven."

"Adam," Junil said, gripping onto the gun, "I love you so much."

"I love you too."

"You were always a brother to me. I don't think I can live without you."

"Just let my will go through." Adam's eyes were devoid of everything essential to the human brain. He felt no emotion, no fear, and had no more will to continue on with his life. These were the eyes of a dead man. "We'll meet in heaven."

"Can't we just run away together?"

Adam pointed to his own forehead. "Two shots, right here. Make them count. After all, William's flames are already going to kill me. I feel them burning my insides."

"Adam, please!" Junil started to cry.

Junil's tears were flooding out of his eyes like running faucets. His face was red. His arms were shaking as he raised them to aim the gun at Adam. All Adam did was watch as Junil struggled to point the gun. Junil's stomach started to turn. He felt sick.

Adam looked at Junil dead in the eyes, grinning. "Our Father, who art in heaven, hallowed be thy name; thy kingdom come, thy will be done on earth as it is in heaven." Junil could barely hold the pistol, but that didn't stop Adam from continuing. "Give us this day our daily bread, and forgive us our trespasses, as we forgive those who trespass against us; and lead us not into temptation, but deliver us from evil. For the kingdom, the power and the glory are yours now and forever."

Two shots reverberated throughout the room. Junil's mind memorized those shots, knowing he would never forget them. On the floor by the apse of the church, Adam's body laid on the ground. All Junil could think about was Adam. Junil dropped the gun and ran over to Adam's corpse. Pain enveloped Junil's soul as Adam passed on into the afterlife. No words could explain Junil's pain.

Adam was gone. Junil lost the closest man to him. Adam made a sacrifice so Junil could live a better life for the second time, but this time, it cost him his own life. Junil could not speak. There was nothing but silence in the church. The silence was destroying Junil as his head started to turn against him. His mind was failing on him.

Junil got on both of his knees and held Adam's body. Teardrops started to fall from Junil's eyes and onto Adam's brown coat. Junil started to twitch. His body felt cold, but above all, he felt impure. He was never going to be the same again after taking the life of his own friend. His eyes were wide as tears flowed out of them. His eyes stopped producing tears and instead they only welled up. The detective closed his eyes, letting the final batch of tears flow down his red face.

Junil let Adam go and stood up again. He clenched his fists and looked down. He slowly started walking across the church nave. He was practically just dragging his feet along. His shoulders felt heavy, his body was in pain, and he would never forget this moment. Junil opened the door outside of the church and had his eyes destroyed by the sun. He covered the sunlight using his hand and fixed his posture.

The despair he felt overwhelmed his sense of justice to defend the civilians of Velindas. Junil was lost. It hit him all at once: he was going to be the greatest detective for taking down Rose. All he had to do was keep living the life that Adam couldn't live.

"I'm glad we could get in here," James said. "I guess everyone already evacuated from the warning for the Blooming Day."

"What was the warning?"

James looked at the security camera to make sure it was disfigured so the center of the Blooming Day couldn't be recorded. "The entire city will burn tonight if I'm stopped. I talked to the business that owned this building about it. He seemed nice."

"Who's going to stop you?" Kaylin asked, unsure what to think of James' actions.

"Find out."

James took a seat in one of the office chairs. He looked out of the window and broke his own silence. "Two stories, huh?"

"And?"

"Might break a bone if you fall."

"We have walls for a reason."

"The walls around us are almost entirely glass."

The room was empty in terms of noise. All that could be heard was ambience and nothing else. Kaylin didn't want to say much, but neither did James. Who were they to blame? For Kaylin, she was confused. On James' shoulders were weights. He was going to have to carry the burden of following through with the Blooming Day.

"Kaylin," James spoke up, "I love you."

"I love you too, James."

"Everything that's about to happen is for you."

Kaylin's voice remained firm. "You know I don't want this, James."

"I have to do this for you."

"Why? Can't you understand that I'm happy the way life is?"

James got up out of his seat and went up to Kaylin. Grabbing her shoulders gently and leaning down toward her face, he finally clarified the why in all of his motives. "You're beautiful, Kaylin. You're the most wonderful person to ever touch the face of the Earth. Mother truly gave birth to an angel. The world needs to see you for who you are."

"I don't need that."

"The world needs that, and so do you. You need to rise up in the world."

"Why couldn't I just do it by myself?"

James let go of Kaylin's shoulders and moved back. "You're weak. You're blind, defenseless, small, and you'll never make it in such an awful world like this."

"But—"

"This world puts people down just for being who they are. Whether they have a cloud or not, who they love, what they were born as, even what they want the future to look like. Nobody can be who they truly want to be."

"What does that mean for you?" Kaylin's question went straight through James' soul.

"This isn't me. I did everything for this moment. Rose was dedicated to you."

"Mom and dad, did you want to do it?"

"I never wanted to kill them. It hurt so bad to see your clueless expression, not knowing your own parents were killed. I can't shake the image out of my head."

"But why would you kill our very own parents?"

"I needed power." James' words gave Kaylin an antsy feeling in her gut. James killed both of their parents only for power.

"The Blooming Day is the culmination of Rose's efforts, and it's all for me?"

"Exactly."

"Liar."

James froze. "I'm not lying."

"If you did everything with me in mind, our parents would still be with us."

James was showing his colors, something he never did toward Kaylin. "Everyone who has died simply passed on for the Blooming Day."

"James, you never had to do this."

"Adam couldn't be who he wanted, and neither could Thirteen. They tried to make their final wills known, Kaylin. And even though Thirteen lives on, there was no way for her to achieve what she wanted to."

Kaylin puffed her chest out. "There's nothing I ever wanted to be besides happy."

"The world never planned on letting that happen."

Kaylin was silent. It was true, Kaylin was never happy. Her

blindness was an obstacle to everything and her small figure made her weak. Kaylin felt walked on all the time. She never saw herself as inferior, but she knew the world never gave her a chance.

James continued, "I'm going to end Kuril's life."

Kaylin broke into the same cold sweat that haunted her at the hospital. "Enough, please."

"I understand how you feel."

"No, you don't."

James went across the room and back to his chair. The office building was completely empty besides the two siblings, but James knew this was going to end up becoming a landmark in history by the end of tonight. James looked over at Kaylin.

"Can I hear you say it again?" James asked.

"Say what?"

"That you love me."

"I love you, James," Kaylin reassured him in fear.

"You're truly an angel."

Kaylin didn't want to respond. The two sat alone in the barely lit office building, filled with anxiety and fear. James took out his phone and called Kuril. It was time to begin the Blooming Day. On the other side of the line, Kuril immediately picked up.

"I saw the warning," Kuril immediately said, "Yanni notified me. This war ends tonight."

"Foxek's Office Building, right by Closedown Avenue. I'm on the second floor alongside Kaylin, please show up."

"Kaylin?"

"She's safe, please don't worry."

Kuril hung up.

James laughed. "He's not a talker."

"He's a sweet guy, just not talkative," Kaylin said.

"Seems like he doesn't need many words."

"I suppose so."

James then called Junil after a few seconds of waiting. The

phone rang for some time. On the other end of the line, Junil finally picked up.

"What is it, James?" There was despair in his voice. It was almost silent, but it was enough for James to hear it.

"The finale for Rose is soon. I ask that you allow Kuril and I to be alone in the building. You, as a detective, are allowed to do whatever you'd like."

Junil didn't respond.

"Can you hear me?" James asked.

"I can hear you."

"I want you to make it known that I'm at Foxek's Office Building by Closedown Avenue. Gather police forces and make sure we have a cushion in case we have a fall."

"Okay."

"Junil, you really are a kind soul. I'm sorry to hear about Adam's passing. It pains me too. It's going to be hard for both of us to live without him."

"Why are you so human, yet so inhumane?"

"I wish I knew myself. Don't enter the building and don't let anyone in for Adam's sake."

"I understand. Best of luck on your end."

Junil hung up. Kaylin, upon hearing James' end of the conversation, decided to bring herself to ask some questions.

"James, who's going to fall?"

"I don't know."

"Why were both of them notified?"

"I don't know."

"What happened to Adam?"

"I don't know."

Kaylin gave up on asking James questions. James stood up and cleared space in the middle of the room, almost as if he needed the whole room for the finale of Rose. He started to stretch a little, then looked over at Kaylin.

"Promise me you'll be okay, Kaylin."

"I don't know what's happening."

"You'll be fine," James said, "but it may hurt for a while. Kuril definitely doesn't deserve this, but it's survival of the fittest."

After around fifteen minutes of waiting in silence, Kuril made his entry. Kuril opened the door from the staircase. His entrance wasn't dramatic, but his eyes were deadly. There was an aura about him that put Kaylin off even though she couldn't see him. In fact, Kaylin had no idea it was Kuril who just came in.

"This ends here," Kuril said.

James looked out the window to see police forces coming together. He smiled, knowing everything was going exactly as he planned.

"Kuril, this is all my plan."

"I'm not going to die."

"That's quick thinking," James replied, "but you're wrong."

Kaylin cut the conversation off. "Why do you two have to kill?" Her tone of voice clearly shifted to one that was filled with fear and confusion.

Kuril's voice was low, but loud. The waiting for his revenge had made him grow impatient. "He killed everyone I knew. You're going straight to Hell, James."

James looked out the window again to see Junil directing a unit of cops. A gathering of people was made around the police, but there was still a gap between the two groups.

"We have a crowd," James said with a grin across his face.

The police rolled out a blanket. One officer grabbed each end and spread it out. If someone fell from two stories, there would be no doubt that they'd be safe. It seemed as if the police were taking all the measures James wanted.

"Kuril," James started, "I apologize for the pain I've put you through."

"That isn't enough. I want you dead."

"Kaylin, stay back."

The two men were about to fight. Years after years of longing for revenge, Kuril finally got to face his enemy in battle. Though the space was closed and not ideal for him, he was dedicated to victory. James on the other hand was only dedicated to finishing the Blooming Day plan.

Kuril cracked his knuckles one by one. James stood still, ready to fight. There was no fire in James' eyes, considering he knew what was going to happen. Kuril, however, had been suppressing his anger ever since he met Junil. He was going to put an end to everything here.

Kuril ran at James with his fist up. James got into his fighting stance and fell back. While Kuril tried to repeatedly throw punches, James' swift movements only blocked them, his arms taking every hit. Kuril threw a punch, but became water as he flung his hit toward James. Reappearing behind James, he attempted to get low and sweep kick him. James easily predicted that it was coming and jumped over the low kick with ease, looking down at Kuril while locking eye contact.

"Please stop fighting!" Kaylin yelled.

The two men didn't even pause. James threw a punch at Kuril's face, a direct hit. Kuril didn't care, he just ate the punch up. The two kept exchanging punches on each other, not even caring to dodge or block any hits. There was glory in those punches, there was frustration in each hit, and every movement came from years of distraught.

Kuril threw one punch at James that caught him off his guard and knocked him into the floor. Pinning him down with his body, Kuril punched James in the face nonstop. Kuril got up and tried to stomp on James' neck in his rage, but the head of Rose rolled over and got up to his feet. Throwing a quarter-punch at Kuril as a fake then hitting him in the gut, James got Kuril to lower his torso for the slightest time for him to take advantage. James grabbed Kuril's hair and threw him into the ground. James felt his body beginning to fail as he caught his breath.

"You're really something," Kuril said, getting up.

"I suppose so."

"I'm not done yet."

Kuril reappeared from behind James. It was the perfect plan: to look like you lost, but get up and take advantage from the back. James looked back at Kuril immediately. It felt like Kuril was always going to be slower than James, who knew every single fighting strategy and was speedy enough to hop over a moving car.

Kuril punched him in the face, which caused him to lose his balance. He didn't even try to dodge it. Kuril brought James to the floor with a kick to the face. James had given up. There was nothing James wanted to do except to let Kuril take his anger out. James was pinned yet again by Kuril, who threw constant punches. In James' eyes, tears formed. He was feeling several emotions, but his mind could not pick one.

"Why do you cry?" Kuril yelled, throwing punches left and right. "Why do you cry when my entire fucking family died by your hand? What reason do you have to even shed a tear?"

"I'm sorry."

"That doesn't fix the fucking wounds you put on my brain— on my people!"

Kaylin screamed, "Kuril, stop!"

Kuril didn't listen. James kicked Kuril up and managed to get to his feet before Kuril could regain his balance. James looked at Kuril with two eyes that were filled with despair, anguish, sorrow, and pain. Kuril saw it too: there was endless negativity in James' eyes.

At that point, Kuril realized the mistake he had made: he looked into James' eyes. Eight figures, which all resembled James, dispersed from James' stature, almost as if he were duplicating himself. The figures of James circled around Kuril. As they all went in to make individual blows, Kuril shut his eyes and liquified, causing the figures of James to phase through each other. The Violet reformed in the air and kicked all of the figures as they intersected. The real James was knocked backward as he grabbed onto his cheek where he was kicked.

The head of Rose smiled. "You're impressive, Kuril."

With a few yards between the two, Kuril stared into James' eyes to show that he wasn't scared.

James rubbed his cheek. "You know, Kuril, you definitely have a good cloud. It surprises me that I have found someone as talented as you."

"I was trained by the best."

"The way you fight, the way you talk, the way you conceal yourself, and the way you utilize your battle intelligence impress me. Adam would've loved you."

Kuril scoffed. "You speak too much."

"Oh? Did you notice what I was doing?"

"What do you mean?"

"Did you notice that you're talking to an illusion?"

Kuril's eyes widened as he felt the presence of James behind him. He had no clue that the James he was talking to was an illusion. James' deadly eyes widened with the intent to kill Kuril from behind. As Kuril felt a switchblade make contact with his back, he became water and reformed after James finished his dash.

The blond man turned to retaliate against James. Looking back, the black-haired forced eye contact with Kuril. Though the deadly glare of James was enough to startle Kuril, the power that the glare had was frightening.

James maintained eye contact. "As of right now, neither of us are the most powerful man alive."

"Who is?"

"Adam."

The Violet immediately caught on. "Adam killed Junil?"

"And as a result, gained a tremendous amount of power."

"Why would you tell me this?"

James' grin reached both sides of his face. "Once I kill you, I will reclaim the title of the world's most powerful man." Kuril fell to his knees, unable to pick himself up. "Then I will kill Adam and become unrivaled."

"You used Kaylin as a means to further your goals. You're disgusting."

"I hope you understand. I have to live. I can't let myself succumb to illness."

"I don't get it."

James chuckled, looking down on Kuril. "I will likely achieve a cloud unlock once I gain that immense power. Due to the nature of a cloud adapting to the user's will, my cloud unlock will save my life."

"I won't let you win."

"My ocular ability to cast illusions is not just for visual effect. All five senses can be corrupted beyond belief. You can't even move your limbs or liquify yourself right now. Did you notice?"

Kuril looked up at the head of Rose. "You said Adam killed Junil?"

"That's right." James smirked. "You look so pathetic on the ground below me."

Kaylin watched on, knowing the truth behind James' words. Adam didn't kill Junil. In fact, Junil had ended Adam's life. Why would James lie?

"Junil isn't dead," Kuril finally replied.

"What makes you say that?"

"He can't be."

James maniacally laughed with a wide-eyed grin. The black-haired individual was showing a side of him that even Kaylin had never seen. He calmed down quickly, focusing back on Kuril. "Why don't you see for yourself in Hell?"

"Junil can't be dead."

James revealed a switchblade from his pocket. "It's not my usual switchblade, but I'm sure this one will work. You had an interesting life, Kuril. Once again, I apologize."

The head of Rose slowly crouched down to Kuril, who was

practically immobile. Even though the Violet didn't struggle, the truth was that James' cloud was overpowering him. There was no doubt that he was the strongest person he had ever met.

Kuril's eyes had lost their color. The aquatic blue color of the Violet, one of the more definable traits of Kuril's people, had left his irises. Still on his knees, he bowed his head. "He can't be."

James grabbed onto Kuril's shoulder. "It must be awful losing the last thing you had in life."

There was a pause, almost as if James was waiting for Kuril to respond. At that time, the entire room was silent. Kuril's despair-ridden face grew more dull each passing moment. The ocean inside of Kuril had relaxed. The waves had stopped crashing onto his own shore. Kuril had nothing more. It was empty.

"Water, unlock."

Kuril's aura became visible. James immediately stood back up and jumped back in shock. Despite still being on his knees with his head down, Kuril had put fear into his enemy. That aura shook the entire room, shifting small objects due to the overwhelming nature of the cloud unlock.

"I'll kill you," the Violet spoke. "I'll kill you!"

From outside of the building, everyone felt the rush of Kuril's cloud unlock. Onlookers talked amongst themselves, slightly backing up as a crowd in fear. Junil watched on, horrified at the amount of power being expended from the building. Deep down, he knew that aura was Kuril's self-destructive tendencies at work. He had remembered the truth of his partner throughout the journey: Kuril did not care if he died.

Yanni rushed over to Junil. "What's going on in there? That aura is insanely strong!"

"It's a cloud user expending all his energy at once."

Looking at the building where the aura originated, Yanni felt an imbalance in his body. "This is a suicide."

"Stay on guard."

Inside of the building, Kuril had finally gotten up. Oddly

enough, Kuril did not have to support his body in order to stand. It was almost as if he had gravitated upward onto his two feet. He looked into James' eyes on the verge of breaking down, yet he had no words to share.

James looked around cautiously, checking for what the cloud unlock's ability could be. Kuril raised his arm to the height of his chest, pointing his hand at James. Snapping his finger, eight spears formed of water appeared around James. He immediately jumped out of the way, barely making it out of the circle of spears. At the same time, the spears all moved inward and collided with each other, a blow that would've put eight different holes in James' body.

"So that's your cloud unlock, huh?" James asked. "You finally got it."

"You will die here, James."

"It's intriguing. The ability to make water out of air and manipulate it? That's just fascinating—"

Kuril snapped. "Shut up."

A spear of water pierced James' side and dispersed, creating a half circle in his body. Stumbling, James caught his balance. He smiled as he gripped onto his knee, breathing heavily.

"Kuril, Junil is alive!" Kaylin yelled. She had been silent this entire time, but she knew she had to interfere once and for all.

"What?" Kuril looked over at Kaylin. "What do you mean?"

"Junil is alive. He killed Adam."

"How do you know?"

"I heard James say it. Please trust me."

Kuril looked back at James, who was struggling to hold himself up. "Is it true?"

The head of Rose looked up, still gripping onto his knee to keep his balance. "Who knows?"

"What are you? A liar?" Kuril yelled.

"I'm a dead man." James looked into Kuril's eyes. "I always have been."

Kuril snapped, sending another spear into James' right arm, which was on the same side of where he was originally pierced. James grunted as the spear lost shape and hit the ground as water after stabbing him.

"Kuril, you have yet to understand who I truly am." James grabbed onto his arm.

"You're a monster."

"Doesn't make me any human."

James ran over at Kuril, his speed being less overwhelming than Kuril remembered. As Kuril stood with his arm out, he snapped. A final, giant spear, gutted James. He fell to the floor as blood spilled out of him.

Behind Kuril was the real James. With a switchblade plunged into Kuril's side, he returned to his senses. James had cast an illusion on him, making him wonder how much was real and how much was fake. Removing the knife, James went to stab him again, but his switchblade plunged into water as Kuril liquified. Reforming at the rear view of James, Kuril punched James' jaw as he tried to look behind him.

Flying back toward the glass windows, James gripped onto his side. Kuril had noticed that no spear had ever pierced James' arm, it was merely an illusion. Despite that, James was still extremely hurt with the hole to the right of his stomach. Kuril grabbed onto the stab wound that James inflicted on him. At this point, Kuril's aura had cooled down, yet he had remained significantly stronger.

"You're going to die, Kuril."

"I'm going to kill you."

The two men rushed at each other as Kaylin could only listen. Fearful, anxious, and scared, she had no clue what to do. She wanted the fight to end, yet she knew it would be hopeless to even try.

"Stop!" Kaylin cried out.

Kuril paused as Kaylin yelled, looking over at her and quickly reflecting on what he had become. Before that reflection could end, Kuril ended up stabbed in his stomach. Yelping in pain, he fell back as James took the switchblade back out and kicked him even farther, making him hit the wall.

James slowly walked over to Kuril. "Now I can finally kill you!"

Kuril could not move. Being wounded in such a spot was not easy to deal with, and as a result, his vision faded as James got closer. He wanted to use more energy, but he found himself drained of the ability to do so.

Kaylin, who had heard James, knew immediately what was happening. She could hear James' breathing get louder as he approached Kuril. She quickly stood up and felt around her pocket and grabbed the switchblade James provided her for self-defense. Pressing the button on the switchblade, the blade was revealed.

"Kaylin, don't!" Kuril yelled.

Charging at James, the blind and fragile girl was right next to the world's most notorious criminal. It felt like she could see him, though she knew she couldn't. She felt strange.

The switchblade dove into James' heart. While she expected him to dodge, she realized that James just took the knife in his chest. She immediately felt sick knowing she stabbed her brother. Losing balance when she collided with James, he fell backward while she kept pushing him toward the wall, unable to stop in her tracks.

Continuing the push, Kaylin broke the glass window behind James. The only expression on James' face was a smile, and only Kuril could see a slight glimpse of it.

The knife went deeper into James' heart, sure to kill him if the police down there didn't. Kaylin fell through the glass window on top of James, the blade still in his heart. There was a blade in Kaylin's heart too: the wound of losing her final family member, the person closest to her, and the big brother she loved.

Falling onto the spread out blanket below them, James' body didn't move. On the blanket were two siblings, torn apart by the world around them. The world they both grew to hate destroyed everything they ever wanted, and now they would never even speak to each other again.

Kaylin was never one to open her eyes because she never felt the need to. For the first time, her eyelids opened and she could see. All she could spot was her brother's dead body right below her. She screamed. Her heart was rapidly beating while her eyes would etch her brother's final smile into her brain. She could finally see, but she couldn't see her brother alive.

Her screams reverberated throughout the entire street. Everyone in the surrounding crowd heard it, but they didn't care. They were celebrating. Everyone in the crowd was celebrating the death of Kaylin's brother, who was a monster to them. He was only a monster.

"We need medical assistance!" Junil yelled, directing the medical branch of officials to get to the duo of siblings immediately.

A few police officers ran into the building, only to see Kuril's body pressed against the floor. He eventually stood up as James' cloud wore off. He slowly walked over to the broken window and looked down at Kaylin hovering over James' corpse.

The crowd continued cheering as James' lifeless body remained on the blanket against the ground, not moving. People were coming together as if Velindas was united and happy for once. That person who united them was Kaylin, who had finished off Rose's leader, the world's most wanted man.

Someone in the crowd tried to make their voice the loudest. "The king is dead!"

"This is what you wanted, isn't it? To unite Velindas under Kaylin and I?" Junil mumbled to himself, almost as if he were talking to Adam's spirit.

The crowd grew larger as more people followed the chant. "The king is dead!"

Rose was no more. Adam and James were gone. The entire city was practically shouting at this point. Everyone was repeating the same chant. It seemed like the business side of the city was finally more vibrant than the party side. While officers were scrambling and Junil was running around leading the police force, there was only one thing that could be heard.

"The king is dead!"

The chants echoed in Kaylin's head as she tried to flush out all her senses. She continued to scream endlessly. She didn't want to see. Kaylin wanted to be blind again. She never wanted her brother to die, but there she was, taking his life with her own hands. She felt disgusting and impure as her body was overcome with grief. As tears rolled down her face, her screaming blended together with her sobs. A single teardrop fell onto James' cheek as she hovered over him. His eyes were already closed. It was over. She stared at her hands as they shook. Her screams were loud, but the chants were suffocating her cries.

"The king is dead!"

CHAPTER X

A week after the death of Adam and James, things were finally calming down. Kaylin and Junil were dubbed heroes among the entire city, one thing that everyone in Velindas could agree on. The two have gone through countless interviews, seeing many stories about how courageous they were in their efforts against Rose. Though the media was still squeezing the topic until it was dry, the city had finally relaxed. Velindas seemed more vibrant than ever, not for the celebration, but for the unity behind the disbandment of Rose. The weather remained the same, some people still discussing the rain that fell a week prior.

Kuril, on the other hand, remained anonymous. He didn't appreciate popularity, so he gave all his credit to Kaylin and Junil. The three of them stuck around each other for the next week as Kuril looked for a job and a place to stay where he would live with Kaylin as her caretaker. Junil, on the other hand, continued his detective work, which was mostly paperwork regarding the disbandment of Rose.

Junil was considered the world's greatest detective of all time after the fall of Rose. His skills only sharpened as he followed through with Adam's will to live the life that the former Rose member couldn't live. He's been given a lot of privileges in Velindas and works directly in his city, though he's received opportunities across the entire world.

In the Zipline bar sat Junil, Kuril, and Yanni. While Junil only clenched onto his classic Martini, Kuril and Yanni gladly took sips of their respective drinks. The junior detective had a Gimlet, while Kuril was drinking a Spritz. Junil stared into his Martini, reflecting upon the death of Adam.

Yanni lightly hit Junil's shoulder. "You've been gloomy, Junil."

"I'm sorry," the detective replied.

"You know what I think?" Kuril butted in.

Junil looked over at Kuril, who sat to his left. "What?"

"You ordered a classic Martini because it's the only drink you know."

"And?"

"It must hurt deeply." Kuril took a sip of his drink and looked at Junil's dreadful expression. "That was Adam's favorite drink, right?"

"How would you know?"

"I saw him drink it once."

Junil circled the top of the glass with his finger. "It was his favorite drink."

"Then drink up," Yanni said.

Both Kuril and Junil put their focus on Yanni. For some reason, it seemed rather outlandish to tell Junil to drink the beverage he bought. Junil looked back at his Martini and lifted it up with his shaking right hand. Taking a few sips, he closed his eyes. He had imagined Adam was with him, teasing him about ordering a classic Martini. When he opened his eyes and placed his drink back down, he looked straight ahead as Kuril and Yanni watched.

The hero of Velindas smiled. "It tastes even better than I remember."

Yanni patted Junil's back. "That's what I'm saying! You have to drink up!"

"By the way, did you gain a cloud unlock on that day?" Kuril asked.

"I didn't," responded the detective.

"I see."

"I feel Adam's power flow through me though. I feel so much more flexible with my abilities."

"I can say the same from after my cloud unlock."

Junil took another slow sip from his Martini with his eyes closed. After the drink made contact with the table again, he looked at Kuril again. "What are you going to be doing now that Rose is gone?"

"I'm moving in with Kaylin. I have to take care of her for quite a bit and show her the ropes around life now that she can see."

"Kaylin being able to see makes me wonder a lot about James."

Kuril rested his head on his hand as he listened to Junil. "How so?"

"If Adam's death was sacrificial, yet he played the villain role for so long, who's to say that James wasn't the same?"

"I don't think we'll ever know."

"Are you okay with that?"

"I'm just glad he's dead."

Junil chuckled. "I get it."

Yanni stared at the television on the wall, watching the news. "Isn't it strange that the police's information department gained a new cloud user right after the disbandment of Rose?"

The detective whispered into Yanni's ear. "That's a former Rose member."

"What?"

"You heard me."

"Why would they—"

Junil interrupted Yanni. "Just let him be."

Yanni paused. "Sure."

Kuril lifted his drink, which averted the eyes of his partners to the glass in the air. "Raise your glasses, boys."

In a second, the trio raised all their glasses. A few reverberating clinks echoed in the room as their glasses collided for a cheer. The trio smiled together, knowing that it was all finally over. They had finally arrived at their destination after a long journey of death, emotion, and endless tension. It was about time they could finally kick back and relax. The Rose had finally withered.

Mia and Kyra went on their own paths together. They didn't care for the mundane affairs regarding Rose and decided to live their lives on their own with each other. The two roamed Velindas a lot, moving into an apartment and settling their lives in the beautiful city.

"Hey, Seven," Mia said over the phone.

"What is it?" Seven replied, holding the phone between his shoulder and ear.

"Where were you on the battlefield against Junil and Kuril?"

Seven got a job working as an intel provider for law enforcement. His identity remained anonymous as part of his deal with the police. His cloud was significant to the Velindas team, but he also refused to analyze the scenes where Adam and James passed away.

"No one really came for me," Seven answered.

"That explains it."

Seven raised an eyebrow. "What?"

"Two told the rest of Rose that you killed yourself."

"Hell no!" Seven yelled over the phone. "Was he trying to protect me or something?"

"Your cloud is useful to the police force and you're defenseless without a gun. I think he wanted you alive."

"I'm pretty strong."

The Violet girl's sigh was so strong it could be heard over the phone. "Sure."

"What are you going to do about that Kuril guy?"

"I don't ever want to see him again."

Seven's little interrogation had no purpose besides satisfying his curiosity. "What happened to killing him?"

"I don't want to anymore. Let's drop this topic."

"Got it."

"Anyways, Kyra and I were wondering if you'd want to come to our place to hang out for some time."

"Who the hell is Kyra?" Seven asked.

"That's Twelve."

"Oh!" Seven laughed. "Guess I might as well tell you that my name is Mitch."

"Alright, Mitch. My name is Mia."

The boy chuckled from the other end of the phone. "It's been years and we only just found out each other's names."

"Yet we always knew who each other were."

"No need to get philosophical on me, Mia."

She chuckled back. "You know where the apartment is," she replied, "come over at noon."

"You got beer?"

"I got beer, but you're not legal." She groaned and paused. "Just keep it a secret."

Mitch smiled behind the phone. "I'll be there."

In her apartment, Abigail laid on her soft mattress, longing for James' touch once again. She shed too many tears over the past week and grew numb. She rolled over, wanting to know what those hands felt like again. The man she loved was dead, and all she could do was just think about him now. It was suffering knowing she could never have him back.

She looked over at James' coat, which was at the other end of the room. When he left her apartment, he didn't bring his coat. Abigail had no idea if it was intentional or if he forgot it. Slowly standing up, Abigail's stance already weakened as her legs were forced to hold up her body. She was taking a physical toll just as much mental. The Velindas model walked over to James' coat and tried putting it on. When she picked up the purple jacket, a piece of paper fell out.

Abigail laid the coat down and picked up the paper. She unfolded the piece of paper to see a block of text. It became very clear to her: James meant to leave his coat behind. She started to read the letter written in blue pen.

To my dearest Abigail,

By the time you see this letter, you're likely grieving over my death. I trust you enough to keep this letter to yourself and share it with nobody, not even Kaylin. This letter is somewhat like a suicide note, but I direct it toward you. Your support throughout my entire life as not only my lover, but as a person, showed me a lot of things about this world. I grew up hating this world for being so unfair, but it was the smile that you possess that made me want to keep pushing. I held you very dearly, and with that, I leave you my coat. I also leave you with one final memory of me: the night we held together. I'm quite the romantic, aren't I? Don't cry too much, but smile, knowing I'm watching you from above. I love you more than you know. If you want to let some tears out, go ahead. I'll be watching you from the heavens, that is if I even make it there... who knows? I'm probably in Hell with Adam right now. Well, scratch that, he was actually Catholic. Maybe I'm in Hell alone. It would honestly suck if I was. At this point, I'm just writing because I don't want to say goodbye. I want to talk to you, but this letter is the last thing I can give to you. Wear my coat with pride, not as a Rose affiliate, but as the woman I loved. I left my personal switchblade in one of the pockets as well, so you can keep that too. Don't do anything drastic. Live the life that I couldn't. I've loved you for years, and I always will. Man, I really can't end letters. I haven't written one in years. If you can, I have one final will. All I want from you is to smile more so I can see that face from wherever I am. It makes me happy when you smile.

I don't want to end this letter, but it seems I'm out of space. I love you, Abby. Thank you.

    Truly yours, and only yours,
    James Kensworth

Abigail finished reading the letter. Her face clenched up as she tried to look away, but her eyes were fixated on the signature. Tears started to flow once again as she sniffled. She slowly folded the letter up and placed it on her vanity. Grabbing the dark purple coat once again, she slipped her arms in the comfortable, soft sleeves. It was a little big for her, but she wore it with a smile. Tears didn't stop rolling down her face, but she forced out a smile for James. She started to cry even harder, but kept her smile on.

She looked at the ceiling, clenching her fists as her arms shook. "Thank you, James."

Abigail fell to the floor in James' purple coat. She started to bawl helplessly, unable to control herself. Her cries became loud as she reached the point of yelling. Grief took over the Velindas model, who still struggled to believe the news of her lover's death.

She held the ends of James' coat, repeating the same phrase again and again, almost as if that coat was James himself. "I love you."

A white dove crossed the window of her apartment, covering the sun for half a second.

At the cemetery, Kaylin prayed at James' grave while on both of her knees. Each day of the week, right before the sun would set, she would visit her brother's grave. Tears rolled down her face as she concluded her prayer. Each time she put her hands together at his grave, she was unable to finish without crying. She opened her eyes to read her brother's name on a piece of stone with a rose carved into it.

"I still love you, James."

She clenched her fists together at her side as she remained on her knees. As she trembled, tears rolled down her face. Bowing her head down and slamming the ground below her, Kaylin broke out into a sob. She began to scream at her brother's grave. Punching the dirt repeatedly, Kaylin continued to let her voice out. As utter despair took over her body, she could only feel powerless before the piece of stone that marked her brother.

The sky was finally getting darker as the red hue of the sky faded out. As she continued to weep, the white dove landed on James' grave.

CPSIA information can be obtained
at www.ICGtesting.com
Printed in the USA
BVHW081930170222
629234BV00006B/487